Rent-a-
Puppy, Inc.

Rent-a-Puppy, Inc.

Richard Boughton

Aladdin Paperbacks

For Georgia, who supplied the love

First Aladdin Paperbacks edition 1995
Copyright © 1992 by Richard Boughton
All rights reserved, including the right of reproduction in whole or in part
in any form

Aladdin Paperbacks
An imprint of Simon & Schuster Children's Publishing Division
1230 Avenue of the Americas
New York, NY 10020

Printed in the United States of America
10 9 8 7 6 5 4 3 2 1

The text of this book is set in 11-pt. Century Expanded.

Book design by Tania Garcia

Also available in an Atheneum edition

Library of Congress Cataloging-in-Publication Data
Boughton, Richard.
Rent-a-Puppy, Inc. / Richard Boughton. — 1st Aladdin Paperbacks ed.
p.   cm.
Summary: Nikki and Tyler encounter both amusing and heart-wrenching
problems when they try running a business renting out puppies in
order to avoid giving them up.
ISBN 0-689-71836-5
[1. Dogs—Fiction.   2. Animals—Infancy—Fiction.   3. Pets—
Fiction.   4. Friendship—Fiction.   5. Business enterprises—Fiction.]
I. Title.
PZ7.B6618Re   1995
[Fic]—dc20   93-41688

Contents

1	Nikki Waits	1
2	Tyler, at Last	4
3	A Brief Search	8
4	Emergency!	11
5	Jinx to the Rescue	16
6	Scene of the Crime	21
7	Love at First Sight	25
8	Six Names for Six Dogs	28
9	Seven Weeks Later	32
10	Woe	37
11	The Plan	41
12	Business Partners	44
13	Preparations	49
14	Yes, We Deliver	53

15 Success!   56

16 The Chase   60

17 Deadline   63

18 Cleanup Time   67

19 Attack   70

20 Business Conference   74

21 Messages   78

22 Lost Dog   83

23 Hope-less   88

24 A Talk with Her Father   92

25 Thanksgiving Morning   97

26 Hope   103

1

Nikki Waits

Nikki Savier paced impatiently on the sidewalk outside the school yard. Five minutes passed. Then ten. Still, Tyler did not appear. He must have been kept after class, Nikki decided. She might have known such a thing would happen. Today of all days!

The longer Nikki waited, the more she worried about her dog, Roxanne, alone in the house and very likely forlorn, afraid and in need of human comforting. Roxie's puppies could be born at any time now. Maybe by the weekend. Possibly even before! Nikki felt she should be home with Rox, seeing to her needs, making certain that her health was secure. Poor Rox had grown to an enormous size over the past month alone. The very sight made Nikki feel keenly uneasy.

Weary of pacing, Nikki sat down on the grass inside the school yard gate and began nervously twisting long strands of her hair around her fingers. The mid-September sun was warm and there was a good smell in the air, a clean, crisp smell of dry leaves and cut grass, but Nikki could not enjoy the weather. Instead, she tried to imagine what Rox might be doing at this very moment. Maybe she had finally decided to try out her new whelping bed, Nikki thought. She and Tyler had constructed the bed out of a large apple crate and they'd placed two soft blankets in the bottom, along with a couple of Roxie's old dog toys. Of course, Rox didn't play with toys much anymore, but they hoped that the sight of the old rubber hot dog and the jingling red ball would give her the idea of what the bed was meant for.

Nikki had wanted to buy new, unchewed toys for the puppies, but Tyler talked her out of this. When it came to money matters, he was famously cautious. "Don't count your chickens, or your puppies, before they're hatched," he'd advised. And Nikki had to admit that he was probably right. Tyler had a talent for making good sense.

Shrugging off her backpack, Nikki took out a book with a picture of a beagle on the front. She and Tyler had been reading the book together whenever they could find the time, but they had not yet finished all of the material on whelping. What would happen if Roxie should decide to have the puppies before she and Tyler were prepared? And then what if complications were to arise?

Nikki shook the thought from her head. She opened the book and began to read, but soon closed the cover, unable to concentrate. It just wasn't the same without Tyler. This was something they had agreed to do together, and Nikki liked it that way. Besides, Tyler was a wizard when it came to dealing with technical material. He ate up big words as easily as gumdrops, and seemed to savor them just as much.

Again, Nikki glanced at her watch, then anxiously gazed at the silent doors of the big brick building. By now almost all the other kids would be halfway home. There were a few eighth graders playing basketball on the outdoor court, but that was all. No one else was in sight.

"Come on," Nikki whispered, narrowing her eyes, willing the doors to open. "Come on, Tyler, come on!"

2

Tyler, at Last

Tyler G. Hubbs emerged from the side door of the school building some twenty-five minutes after the dismissal bell had rung.

As he walked across the playground, Tyler considered the offense for which he had been detained. All he had done was tell Ms. Frinke one of the assignments she had given was too juvenile for the sixth grade. In Tyler's opinion, he was too old to be fooling around with shoe boxes and crayons and Elmer's glue. He wanted to learn more important things. Like economics, for instance, or business law. Subjects a guy could sink his teeth into, without getting paste and glitter all over his lips. Ms. Frinke should have accepted his honest objection and excused him from doing the assignment. Instead, she became angry and kept him after class.

By the time Tyler looked up from the plodding toes of his Reeboks he was almost to the fence at the far end of the playground. There, by the open gate, stood Nikki Savier. She was smiling brightly and her jet black hair was all mussed by the gusty breeze.

Briefly, Tyler's lips stretched upward. There was

something about the sight of Nikki's face that made him feel . . . well, he wasn't quite sure how it made him feel. Good, in an odd sort of way. Happy, for no reason in the world. He had been friends with Nikki Savier nearly as long as he could remember. In the past she'd been almost like a sister to him—for Tyler himself was an only child. But in the last year or so something new had begun to happen. He'd begun to notice things he'd never noticed before—silly little things, like the ribbons in her hair, the clothing she wore, the shape of her nose and how it had a little crook at the top. It didn't make a bit of sense, and Tyler Hubbs did not care for things that did not make sense.

Therefore, he forced his smile into a frown and he rolled his eyes tiredly upward.

"What are you doing here?" he said, walking swiftly onward.

"I've been waiting for about a million years." Nikki ran to catch up. "What did you do wrong this time?"

"It was a silly, juvenile assignment, that's all," Tyler grumbled in reply.

"And that's exactly what you told Ms. Frinke, right?" Nikki found herself hard-pressed to stifle a giggle. Tyler's bluntness rarely failed to amuse her. She stayed at his side and kept pace, step for step. At last, Tyler slowed down, and Nikki breathed with relief. Without speaking, they kicked at the fallen leaves as they walked.

Upon reaching the corner of Maple, Tyler stepped off the curbing and started across the street.

"Wait!" Nikki cried, surprised. "Aren't you coming over to see how Rox is doing?"

Tyler stopped in midstride. Wrapped in his dark mood, he had forgotten about Rox. Instantly, his spirits brightened. Tyler had no pets of his own, but he liked to think of Rox as almost his dog—just as he liked to think of Nikki as almost his sister. Smiling openly for the first time, he returned to Nikki's side and they headed toward her house at a quickened pace.

Just as they reached the front steps, Nikki's brother, Jinx, came squealing down the walkway between the holly hedges, startling both Nikki and Tyler. He tripped over a small crack in the pavement and sprawled headlong into Tyler's arms, yelping as Tyler grunted at the impact.

Jinx's real name was Jeffrey, but Nikki had called him Jinx ever since he had learned to hold his own silverware. That was when accidents had begun to happen. Things had a way of leaping out of his pudgy little fists and landing just about anywhere, often in Nikki's lap. Nikki had once calculated that in an average week Jinx would spill ten out of twenty glasses of milk. A fifty percent disaster rating, she called it.

There had been a time, in Jinx's younger years, when Nikki would never have imagined he would grow into such a nuisance. She had held him in her arms and fed him bottles of milk and he'd been so cute and harmless back then. Why do little kids have to grow up? she wondered, sometimes quite bitterly. She missed having a baby to nurture and love. She missed the little infant who could not talk back.

But Jinx was five now, and bored. He attended kindergarten in the morning, but wanted to go to school all day instead of spending the endless afternoon hours next door at Mrs. Zenner's house.

"You're late, Nikki," Jinx accused in a shrill, grating little voice as he disentangled himself from Tyler's arms. His small face was flushed with a glow of sheer mischief. "I'm telling Mom you had to stay after school."

"You'd be lying if you did," Nikki countered. "Do you want me to tell Mom you've been lying?"

"No," Jinx answered emphatically, clearly puzzled over the logic of this, but certain that he did not want his mother to think him a liar.

"Then keep quiet and don't bother us," Nikki warned. "We've got to take care of Roxie now."

The three climbed the steps to the porch. Nikki fished in her pocket for her door key, slid it in the lock, and turned the knob. The door swung open on a dim and silent hallway.

Too silent, Nikki knew at once. Something was definitely wrong.

3

A Brief Search

In the first place, Roxie wasn't barking. Usually she would begin to bark the moment she heard footsteps on the porch. More telling than this, however, was the fact that she hadn't come bounding to the door. Now that was odd. Rox was mad about meeting members of her family. And although she was too fat, these days, to bound very well, she still always managed to rush to the hallway and whirl heavily about like a happy hurricane. Rox wouldn't miss that kind of fun for the world. Unless . . .

Stepping into the hallway, Nikki listened and heard only the distant ticking of a clock. She glanced over her shoulder at Tyler and lifted her palms.

"Where's Rox?" she said.

"Strange," Tyler agreed, wrinkling his brow. "I was just about to ask the same question."

"Rox?" Nikki called. "Roxie?"

There was no answering bark. Not a single sound.

Nikki led the way into the dining room. They did not find Rox there. Nor could they find her in the kitchen, the living room, or either of the two upstairs bedrooms. The whelping bed was vacant as well.

"She's disappeared," Nikki said.

Tyler tapped her shoulder. His eyes were fixed on the door at the end of the hallway.

"No, she wouldn't go in there"—Nikki glanced skeptically at the open door of her father's study—"she knows she's not supposed to."

This was the room where Mr. Savier, a history professor at the university, worked on his biography of Napoléon Bonaparte. He had been laboring on this pet project for the last two years, and he was the only person allowed in the room.

"Rox doesn't always do just what she's supposed to do," Tyler observed.

"Maybe she wanted to go outside, and no one was home, so she jumped out a window," Jinx suggested.

"In the first place, the windows are closed," Nikki said. "And in the second place, we're on the second floor, lame-o."

"Maybe she forgot that, and then broke her legs when she hit the ground," Jinx earnestly persisted.

"Yeah, then maybe she crawled to a phone booth and called for an ambulance," Tyler added, poking Nikki in the ribs with his elbow.

"Would you two knock it off!" Nikki snapped. "Come on, we might as well check it out."

As she led the way down the hall to the study, Nikki silently prayed that Rox had not gone into this room, for her father would be very angry. She had been hoping all along, through the three months of Roxie's pregnancy, that she would be able to keep the puppies when they came. Of course, her parents had told her from the outset that she could not keep them. One dog was more than enough, they'd said, especially when the dog in question was Rox. But Nikki was banking on the actual sight of the puppies, and on the hard work she planned to do in caring for them, to soften her parents and sway them in her favor. She had a picture in her mind of how it would be: she, Nikki Savier, the proud parent of puppies. Rox, like Jinx, had grown up and grown away. Nikki wanted puppies, cute little things that would want to be loved.

Her plan would definitely be off to a horrible start if Rox were to decide to birth her offspring in her father's personal, private study.

As she reached the end of the hallway, Nikki heard a rustling and then a thumping from within the room. She pushed open the door, then froze in her footsteps.

They had found Roxanne. She was crouching alertly in the center of the room. The hair on the back of her neck stood erect. Her brown eyes burned with fear and menace. Her lips were curled in a ragged snarl above her two white rows of long, sharp teeth.

4
Emergency!

Nikki raised her arm in front of Tyler's chest.

"Stop . . . back up," she said. "It's you, Tyler. She's looking at you."

"Me? Why me?" Tyler objected. "Rox knows me."

Rox growled lowly, deep in her throat. She sounded like a car in need of muffler repair.

"Come on, Roxie—what's the matter?" Tyler coaxed in a high, sweet voice. He was aware of sounding silly, but he would do anything just now, even stand on his head, if he thought it would help him regain Roxie's trust.

Rox growled more ominously. She took a threatening step forward, ready to spring.

"Nikki, I'm scared," Jinx whined, scrambling behind Tyler and clutching his belt. "Rox has gone loony."

"No she hasn't," Nikki said. "She's upset, that's all. I was afraid this would happen. Poor Rox has been alone here all day, and now she's afraid and confused. You'd better leave the room, Jinx. You too, Tyler."

"All right, I'm going," Tyler pouted as he backed out

the doorway, nearly stumbling over Jinx in the process. "Boy, that's gratitude for you. After all I've done for that dog."

"She doesn't mean anything by it," Nikki said. "Just give me some time to calm her down."

Tyler grumbled as he retreated down the hallway with Jinx tagging behind like a new-grown tail. At the top of the stairway, he looked back at Nikki, and a queasy sort of concern for her rushed through his heart. Don't be stupid, he told himself. She can handle this.

Nikki remained in the doorway, talking quietly to Rox. She glanced at Tyler and waved her left arm sharply. "Go on!" she whispered.

Feeling suddenly foolish, Tyler thumped down the stairs, shoving Jinx along in front of himself as if he were an unwieldy bag of laundry.

Hardly had Tyler reached the bottom of the staircase when a bloodcurdling shriek pierced the air, setting every nerve in his body on its toes.

"*Tyler!*" Nikki screamed. "Tyler! Help me!"

At once, Jinx jumped three feet in the air. His hair stood as straight as the bristles on a wire brush, and he clung so tightly to Tyler's belt that Tyler had to grab the front of his jeans to keep them from falling down.

"Let go of me!" he demanded, dragging Jinx back to the stairway.

"Don't go up there!" Jinx pleaded at the top of his tiny lungs, digging his heels into the carpet. "Please, I don't want to see it!"

"See what?" Tyler shouted in exasperation.

"Tyler!" Nikki cried again, her voice shrill with panic. "Tyler, hurry—help me—help me!"

"*Mom!*" Jinx wailed.

"Your mother is not home," Tyler answered between his teeth, and groaned as he hauled Jinx onto the third step from the bottom. Suddenly the young boy seemed as heavy as a washing machine.

"I'm calling Dad, then!" Jinx declared. Trembling, he let go of Tyler's belt and flew across the hall to the telephone.

Finding himself suddenly free of Jinx's stubby little fingers, Tyler raced up the stairway, two steps at a time, his heart pumping like a jackhammer.

He found Nikki on her knees in the study, cradling Roxanne's head in her lap. Nikki's face was pasty white, as if she'd just seen a ghost, and Tyler's own face went pale and cold as new snow. If anything had happened to Nikki, he could never forgive himself for having left her alone in the room.

Then he saw it. On the floor about three feet behind Rox lay a very small, black puppy. Between the two, like a long, fat earthworm, stretched the umbilical cord, still intact and attached to both mother and puppy.

"What's that?" Tyler said, stopping abruptly in the doorway as Roxie exposed her gleaming incisors. "Where did this puppy come from?"

"It came from Rox, you dolt!" Nikki answered, suddenly angry for reasons beyond Tyler's comprehension. "It was behind her all along and we didn't even see it! She must have dragged the poor thing across the floor when she heard us coming."

"But she's supposed to take care of it," Tyler argued pointlessly. "She's supposed to be biting off the umbilical cord. It says so in the book!"

13

"Well, what do you want me to do—bite it off myself?"

"Just keep your head," Tyler instructed as evenly as he could manage.

"But what are we going to do?" Nikki pressed. Her voice broke as she looked helplessly from Roxanne to Tyler. Her eyes brimmed with tears.

"I'm sure there's something about this in the book," Tyler replied. Maintaining a calm attitude for Nikki's sake, he left the room in search of her backpack.

When he returned to the study, he found Nikki rocking nervously back and forth, petting Roxie's head. Tyler flipped through the pages of the book, scanning the print as quickly as he could.

"Here it is," he muttered, reading on. Slowly, his face turned pale again. He looked up from the book. "Uh, do you have a big pair of scissors around here?" he asked.

"Scissors?" Nikki gulped.

"The book says you need something sharp. Like a big pair of scissors. It says you have to cut the cord yourself if the dog won't do it."

Nikki closed her eyes. She felt a bit woozy.

"Jinx," she choked. "Jinx, bring me Mom's big scissors. Quick!"

Jinx did not answer.

"He's probably calling your dad," Tyler said.

"What?"

"Never mind. I'll find the scissors myself."

Nikki listened as Tyler's feet thumped down the hallway. She continued to rock Roxie's head in her lap, counting the passing seconds. At last, Tyler reappeared.

Nikki stared with wide, frightened eyes at the long silver blades in his hand. He held the scissors toward her.

"Tyler . . . I can't do it," she admitted with a shudder. "I just can't."

"One of us has to," Tyler answered. "If we don't cut the cord, the puppy could die."

Nikki shook her head and closed her eyes. A single tear made its way to her chin.

Tyler swallowed hard as he looked at Rox and the puppy. I've got to do something, he told himself. Rox stared back at him with confused, fearful eyes. He dropped to his knees.

Slowly Tyler reached out until he could gently touch Rox's head, just above those troubled eyes. He realized at once that this gentle gesture might be his ticket to regaining Roxie's trust.

"Nice old Roxie," he crooned.

Again, Rox bared her teeth. But in a moment her body seemed to relax slightly and draw even closer around Nikki's lap, just long enough to allow Tyler to perform the operation on the umbilical cord. Now was the moment for him to act.

Tyler glanced at Nikki and flashed a reassuring grin. He placed the open book on the floor and studied the pertinent paragraph one more time. He opened the scissors. They felt cold in his hand.

Tyler took a deep breath to settle his nerves, then lowered the blade toward the tiny dog's stomach.

5

Jinx to the Rescue

The moment Tyler touched the scissors to the cord, an amazing thing happened. Rox craned her neck toward him, nudged his hand aside with her snout, and began nipping at the cord herself, right up close to the puppy's skin.

Tyler and Nikki watched in wonder, relieved beyond words. They would not have to use the scissors after all. In no time, Rox had done the job. The umbilical cord was severed. Immediately, her long tongue went to work, massaging the puppy from head to toe to get the blood flowing properly.

"It's just like the book says!" Tyler exclaimed. "Rox knew what to do all along."

The tiny puppy began to wiggle energetically and it whined in a funny, raspy voice.

"Look at how tiny it is," Nikki said, her eyes sparkling.

"And gooey," Tyler added, gulping as he watched Rox clean the puppy. Until now, he had expected that puppies would be born exactly as they appear in pet shop windows—dry and clean and much larger than this one.

Neither Nikki nor Tyler took the least notice of the police siren that wailed down Maple Street, then died directly in front of the house. They were much too involved with Rox and the puppy to be aware of anything outside the four walls of the study. Only when Rox suddenly tensed herself and began to growl again did they realize that something was amiss. Roxie's ears snapped to attention. Her bloodshot eyes widened with alarm.

"What is it?" Nikki and Tyler said together.

Before they knew what was happening, Rox was on her feet. She snatched up the puppy by the scruff of its neck, rushed into the closet, flung the puppy on the floor, and flopped down on top of it.

"Rox, what are you doing!" Tyler exclaimed. "You're going to crush the poor thing!"

"Listen," Nikki said, grabbing Tyler's elbow. "Someone's coming up the stairs."

Tyler heard it too—the sound of footsteps thumping dully on the carpet.

"It must be Jinx," Nikki hopefully suggested.

"Jinx and what army?" Tyler replied.

The two bolted to their feet as the sounds of the footsteps reached the top of the stairway and proceeded down the hall. Slowly, the door swung open and the faces of two policemen peeped in. One of the policemen was so tall that his head fit nicely right on top of his partner's. They stared at Nikki and Tyler as if they'd never seen children. Next, Nikki's father's head nudged itself into the stack made by the two policemen's heads. His eyes, behind the thick lenses of his horn-rimmed glasses, were

17

wide with worry. Finally, Jinx's round, pasty face appeared far below the others.

"Hi," Nikki said, staring with dumb bemusement at the stack of four heads. "What's up?"

With a stupefied expression on his face, Mr. Savier gazed from Nikki to Tyler. He seemed to be looking for something, and not finding it. Finally, he turned his eyes on Jinx.

"Jinx, what's going on here?" he demanded. "I thought something horrible must be happening from what you told me on the phone."

"Horrible!" Jinx echoed shrilly. "S-scissors! T-t-teeth! Mad d-d-d-dog!"

Jinx's mind was helplessly atremble with visions of gnashing white dog teeth and gushing, crimson blood. Ever present was the picture of Roxie's angry face, her curled lips and quavering, wolfish tongue. In his panic, Jinx had hardly been able to speak when he called his father on the telephone. Long ago, Rox had lightly bitten Jinx when he tried to saddle her with the doormat and ride her like a horse. Jinx had never quite gotten over the incident. It had imprinted itself on his memory like an ugly tattoo. But what scared him most of all, just now, were the half-angry, half-confused expressions on the faces surrounding him. Jinx began to cry.

"D-d-dog," he repeated morosely. "T-t-teeth. S-s-scissors . . ."

"Now, calm down, son," Mr. Savier soothed.

The tall policeman placed a hand on the butt of his revolver.

"Just what sort of dog are we talking about here?" he inquired. "Pit bull? Doberman? German shepherd?"

"B-b-beagle," Mr. Savier stammered, then slapped his forehead. "Now he's got me doing it!"

"Where is the d-dog?" the officer pursued. Quickly, he cleared his throat and glanced sheepishly at his partner.

"Yeah," the shorter man added, grinning. "Where is the b-b-beagle?"

Nikki and Tyler looked at each other. Nikki crossed her eyes. Tyler raised one eyebrow.

"The b-b-beagle is in the c-c-closet," Tyler informed the officers in their own odd manner of speaking. "Having p-p-puppies."

Nikki couldn't help but laugh. The policemen laughed also. They straightened up, shrugged their shoulders, and strode into the room, followed by Mr. Savier. Jinx remained in the doorway, ready to flee should Rox suddenly reappear and renew her attack.

"Where did she bite you, Nikki?" he asked.

"She didn't bite me at all," Nikki answered. "What makes you think she bit me?"

The two policemen snickered and winked at one another. Mr. Savier's face darkened. His hand was buried in the breast of his coat. Having studied Napoléon Bonaparte for so long, he had unconsciously fallen into the habit of striking the French emperor's most famous pose.

"What in the world is going on here?" he asked. There was not the least hint of amusement in his voice.

"We told you," Nikki answered. "Rox is having puppies, Dad. Well, she's had one anyway. Look!"

Nikki, Tyler, Mr. Savier, and the two policemen approached the open closet. They gathered in a semicircle and gazed down at Rox.

"I don't see any puppies," Mr. Savier said.

But from beneath Roxie's large, round stomach a strange, muffled noise could be heard. It sounded like a cry for help from the depths of a dark, empty well.

6

Scene of the Crime

"Rox, would you move?" Nikki cried, tugging at Roxie's collar. "You're going to smother your new puppy."

"Why in the heck is she lying on it?" Tyler wondered, straining to lift her rear end.

"Maybe she's trying to protect it," Nikki suggested.

"What—by smashing it?"

At last, Tyler lifted Rox high enough to allow Nikki to reach under and grab the puppy. She brought it out very gently and held it in both hands for everyone to see.

Mr. Savier and the policemen crouched in the center of the room as Nikki placed the puppy on the floor in front of them. Each reached out and took a turn at petting the tiny dog. They petted it very lightly, using only the tips of their fingers. The puppy wormed about in wobbly circles, its eyelids tightly closed, as they would be for weeks to come. It was a miracle, Nikki thought— the miracle of birth—and it had happened right before her eyes. It filled her with joy, and she looked at Tyler and saw that he too was joyful and amazed.

Rox struggled to her feet and prowled forward from

the closet. She growled once, then turned her eyes shyly from face to face, overwhelmed by the army of onlookers.

"Take it easy," Tyler said, rubbing the fur on her neck. "No one's going to hurt you."

"Or your puppy," Nikki added, kneeling beside Tyler.

"Oh, no!" Mr. Savier suddenly croaked, shattering Nikki's mood. "What has Rox done to my closet?"

No one had noticed, until now, the mess Rox had made in the little room. Mr. Savier's favorite tweeds and gabardines were spread on the floor in jumbled heaps. His shirts were strewn about like tattered flags on a battlefield.

"Look," Nikki exclaimed, fascinated, "Rox has made her own whelping bed!"

"Using only the finest materials," the tall policeman commented, chuckling under his breath.

"Ugh!" Mr. Savier groaned, slapping his forehead once again. "My suits!" he lamented miserably. "My dress shirts, my neckties!"

"It's not her fault, Dad," Nikki claimed in Roxanne's defense. "She was only following her instincts."

"Instincts, my foot!" Mr. Savier began—but then another, greater horror entered his mind.

At once, he rushed to the closet and threw himself on his knees amid the rumpled clothing.

"My research!" he gasped. "Where is my research!"

Mr. Savier was referring to the bundles of notes he had collected for his biography of Napoléon Bonaparte. Hundreds of pages had been stored in five plastic baskets in the back of the closet.

Feverishly, he tunneled his way through the shambles, shoveling clothing between his legs as a dog would shovel dirt. At last, his fingers gripped the plastic edge of one of the baskets. As he pulled the basket into the light, his face went blank and his mouth dropped open. Writhing atop the crinkled nest of paper in the basket was another little puppy. This one was white, with a single tan patch on its rump. Its snout was completely furless and the skin was pink. The puppy was wet—and so was Mr. Savier's research.

In a daze, he rose to his feet, holding the creature away from the basket as he stared, aghast, at the jumbled, discolored stack of paper.

"Dad!" Nikki exclaimed. "Where did you get that dog?"

Momentarily shocked beyond the capacity to speak, Mr. Savier merely stared vacantly at the puppy, as if it had simply appeared in his hand like a magician's white dove.

"Well, it's not mine!" he finally protested.

"Listen!" Nikki said. She crawled to the closet and held a hand up for silence.

From within the dark interior came the sounds of several tiny voices, whimpering and whining. It sounded for all the world as if her father's suits were whispering secrets among themselves.

"There are more puppies in there!" Tyler howled excitedly.

Instantly, he and Nikki dove into the closet, snatching up the scattered garments and tossing them out the door. The two policemen stood by, helpfully catching the garments and folding them over their arms. Mr. Savier looked on in utter dismay.

"Here's another basket," Nikki shouted. "*And* another puppy!"

"Two . . . three!" Tyler added, pulling out the baskets, each with its own small passenger, and sliding them in the direction of the helpful officers.

"Four!" Nikki cried. "That makes six altogether, counting Dad's and the black one. Rox has made beds of all these little baskets! She's had six puppies, and we thought she'd only had one!"

Mr. Savier gathered the baskets in front of himself. He removed the puppies, one by one, from the comfy cribs Rox had made of his two years' worth of research. His eyes, burning with aggravation, fell upon Rox. Again, his hand found its way into the breast of his blazer.

Cringing, Rox backed toward a corner and made a futile attempt at hiding herself behind a coat tree. An apologetic grin arched across her long, pink lips.

7

Love at First Sight

So it happened that the policemen whom Jinx, in his hysteria, had caused his father to summon came in handy after all.

Each officer dropped his bundle of clothing and stepped in front of Mr. Savier as he started toward Rox.

"Now hold on, sir," the tall one said. "You don't want to lose your temper over this."

"Yes," his short partner added. "Take it easy, please. It wasn't the beagle's fault."

"That's right, Dad," Nikki quickly agreed. "Rox was only doing what she thought was right."

For a moment longer Mr. Savier clenched his fists, and his jaw moved back and forth. Nikki could actually hear the grinding of his teeth. At last he opened his palms. His shoulders slumped forward in defeat.

"Two long years of hard work," he moaned. "Two long years."

"Come on, Dad," Nikki said, "it's not all that bad." She picked up one of the baskets and took some of the papers out. "You can still read what the notes say. They're just a little wet, that's all."

"And a little gooey," Tyler added.

Mr. Savier raised a hand and covered his eyes. "Please take me out of here," he pleaded. "I can't stand to see any more."

The two officers ushered Mr. Savier from the room, patting his shoulders sympathetically even as they chuckled softly behind his back. Before returning to their patrol car, they came back to the study to pet and admire the puppies once more.

"Sorry to have bothered you," Nikki said to the officers. "My little brother has a bad habit of overreacting."

Jinx, who had disappeared for a time, now reappeared in the doorway and stood bashfully behind the policemen, fascinated by their uniforms and handcuffs and guns.

"No problem," the tall officer answered, winking at Nikki, then smiling at Jinx. "Call us any time."

"Yes, unless your next pet happens to be a pregnant grizzly bear," the short officer added.

With that, they waved and went back to their duties.

Nikki and Tyler looked at one another. Slowly, they smiled. The room was quiet at last, suddenly as full of peace as it had been of commotion.

Rox had returned to her comfy bed in the closet, and the sightless puppies had each made their way to a teat, from which they took their first sucks of milk, gurgling like six little coffeemakers. Rox cleaned each puppy a second time, then a third.

"If she doesn't let up, she's gonna drown them," Tyler said.

"Don't worry about Rox," Nikki told him. "She knows what she's doing."

"Yeah, like when she stuffed them all in the back of the closet and then lay on top of 'em," Tyler answered, laughing. "That's what I call brainy, all right."

"She was hiding them," Nikki objected. "She was protecting them from . . . from *predators*."

"Hah," Tyler scoffed. "Some predators we are."

But Nikki ignored her friend's doubtful attitude. She was completely amazed at the perfection of Roxie's instincts. All alone, she had birthed six puppies. Filled with a feeling of awe and warmth, Nikki crawled into the closet with Rox and the puppies. Rox glanced up out of weary eyes and allowed Nikki to curl up beside her. And as the puppies fell sleepily, one by one, from Roxanne's teats, Nikki scooped them up and cradled them lovingly.

Small and helpless, the puppies nuzzled close and seemed to need Nikki as much as they needed Rox. Nikki marveled at the feel of their solid yet fragile little bodies, suddenly so real after having been hidden so long within Roxie's womb. Carefully, as if she were handling crystal vases, she returned the puppies to the warm fur of Roxie's stomach.

And Nikki Savier knew, more surely than ever, that she could not bear to part with a single puppy. Together, she and Rox would take care of them and watch them grow.

"These really will be my children," Nikki whispered, smiling upon the brood. "Each and every pup."

8

Six Names for Six Dogs

By dinnertime, Nikki's father had calmed himself somewhat. He sat quietly at the table with his family. Tyler and Mrs. Hubbs had been invited as well. For a time, no one mentioned Rox or the puppies.

At last, Nikki offered a quiet suggestion.

"Can we name the puppies after dinner?" she asked.

"No point in giving them names," her father answered quickly, glancing up from his baked potato. "That would only strengthen a bond that will have to be broken."

Nikki cringed, but forced herself to remain calm and confident. She knew it would take time to convince her parents to let her keep the puppies. She needed to be patient and persistent, that was all.

"But they have to stay here for at least seven weeks," Nikki countered in a matter-of-fact tone of voice. "Puppies can't leave their mother before they're weaned. And they won't even open their eyes until two weeks have passed, or start on solid food for a month. It won't hurt to name them, Dad. Really, it won't."

Nikki imagined that her father's expression softened for just a moment, and she felt suddenly certain she could change his mind, if only given a chance and some time. She and the puppies would have seven long weeks to work on him. Surely in that amount of time the little dogs would be able to endear themselves so completely that not even the greatest ogre in the world would be able to send them away.

"Just where are these puppies going to stay while they're here?" Mr. Savier asked, gazing thoughtfully at his spoonful of peas.

"Right where they are," Mrs. Savier told him.

"Where—in my study?"

"Exactly," she answered. "I won't have them racing around the house like a pack of wild . . . well, like a pack of wild puppies."

"But what will happen to my work? What will happen to Napoléon?"

"Don't worry, Dad," Nikki jumped in, having anticipated her father's concern. "Tyler and I will move your things to another room—your desk, your papers, your books—everything. And we'll clean the study every day, and never let the puppies loose in the house."

Nikki's father grumbled to himself. He dropped his spoon and pushed his plate aside.

"So can we, Dad?" Nikki repeated. "Can we name the puppies?"

"I still don't think it would be a good idea," he stated. "Honestly, Nikki, I don't."

Nonetheless, when dinner was finished the Saviers and their guests gathered in the study. They sat down on the floor and petted Rox and her children, snuggled together in their closet fortress.

"Oh, you're happy, aren't you?" Nikki's father said to Rox. "I'll bet you're just as pleased as punch."

Rox winked a friendly eye and lifted one ear.

Mr. Savier scowled, but then smiled despite himself.

Of Roxie's six puppies, three were male and three female. Nikki reached into the furry crowd and picked up the white-and-tan dog her father had discovered in the first plastic basket.

"Well," she pondered, narrowing her eyes, "what would be a good name for you?"

"How about Killer," Jinx offered.

"Don't be stupid, she doesn't even have teeth yet!" Nikki glared hotly at her brother. "Besides, you can't name a girl dog Killer."

"I found it—I name it," Mr. Savier declared, folding his arms and raising his chin. His eyes seemed to glow with reenlivened memories of the afternoon's disastrous events. "Catastrophe," he decided and flashed a roguish grin. "That dog will be called Catastrophe."

"That's no name for a puppy, Dad," Nikki said.

"It's my choice," he insisted. "I found the dog first."

"Okay, have it your way," Nikki said. But she whispered so that all could hear, "We'll call her Caddie for short."

The next choice was Tyler's. He gave the name Albert Einstein to a furry, brown male with an intelligent-looking face.

Mrs. Savier chose Cubby for a skinny, tan male and Jinx named one of the females Sugar Baby, after his favorite sort of candy.

Tyler's mother named the fifth puppy Bluto because, as she explained, he was so large and robust.

Lastly, Nikki picked up the small black puppy which Roxanne, in the throes of her earlier panic, had dragged across the floor. This, a female, was the runt of the litter. Its body felt damp and limp in her hands, and Nikki's heart went helplessly out to the little animal. From time to time its chest would convulse as the pup took in sudden, tense breaths, as if gulping bravely for every bit of air it could get.

The room fell silent as Nikki cradled the weak pup to her chest. No one offered a name, and Nikki knew the meaning of their silence. They were thinking that this puppy might not live.

Nikki turned the pup carefully in her hands and looked closely at its face—the little snout so wrinkled and pudgy, the eyes pressed close like rosebuds in winter.

No, you won't die, she said in her mind—and her words were a promise to herself as well. You're going to grow up alongside your brothers and sisters and run and play and be healthy and happy. I'll force you to do it if I have to!

Nikki closed her eyes, as if making a wish. She kissed the tip of the puppy's nose.

"Hope," she said at last, smiling courageously from face to face. "This puppy's name will be Hope."

9

Seven Weeks Later

The next seven weeks were the happiest weeks of Nikki's life. She and Tyler spent every available hour caring for the puppies and watching them grow from the helpless, crawly little creatures they had been on their first day in the world into strong, rambunctious, bright-eyed little hounds.

For Nikki, the miracle of the puppies' birth did not fade with that first day, but continued through each day after as they grew ever more strong and lively, gained their own feet, discovered their muscles, their teeth, their small, shrill voices. Each pup grew into its name like a caterpillar into a butterfly, so that very soon Cubby could not have been mistaken for Caddie, nor Sugar Baby for Albert Einstein, nor Bluto for Hope. Tyler taught them to come when he called their names. They were smart little puppies and seemed to learn a hundred new things every day.

The task of caring for the puppies was as much a part of Nikki's and Tyler's lives as going to school or sleeping at night, and more enjoyable, by far, than either. As the puppies' teeth grew, Rox became sore from giving milk. Therefore, the two humans stepped in to help in the weaning process, feeding the pups warm milk from teaspoons. When a week of cold weather set in, they kept the puppies warm by installing a space heater next to their box. They kept them well fed so that each pup would grow strong and husky.

At night when the puppies wakened Nikki with their chorus of wailing for attention, she would stagger out of bed and wander with half-opened eyes down the dark hallway and wonder, for a moment, whether this was worth her trouble after all. But at last, when she'd managed to quiet the brood and had gotten them back to sleep in their box, a feeling of pride and accomplishment would soothe her weary bones—just the same, she thought, as a parent of human children would feel—and Nikki would know again, more surely than ever, that she must be doing the right thing.

True to her promise, Nikki single-handedly nursed Hope to good health by constant administerings of vitamin tablets, broken into tiny pieces, pinches of sugar in her milk, blankets for added warmth at night, and most of all, sheer determination. At last Hope was as boisterous and healthy as her siblings, and her fur turned color from a lusterless black to a beautiful silver-gray sheen.

So it happened that Nikki quickly grew most fond of this particular puppy. Hope seemed almost her own creation, like a wilting flower one might save from a frost and, with loving care, cause to bloom and be bright. Hope was the first puppy to open her eyes—for, no doubt, she wanted to see who this constant companion of hers could be. She blinked at the morning sunlight coming through the study window, and gradually her dark eyes, black and shiny as opals, focused on Nikki's face.

Nikki drew in a breath of astonishment. She wanted to call out for Tyler to come see, but feared if she were to speak too loudly, Hope might change her mind and close her eyes again. Therefore, Nikki merely gazed back into Hope's eyes, and in them perceived the first light of love.

"I am for you," those radiant eyes seemed to say. "And you are for me."

Nikki knew at that moment that they must never be parted. Whatever happened, they must stay together.

Through the weeks, Nikki concentrated on dropping subtle hints here and there to her parents. She pointed out, for instance, how very quiet the puppies had been the night before. "You'd hardly even know they were here," she said. And sometimes she would carry a puppy from the study and set it on her mother's or her father's lap, so that they could pet the little dog and see how nice and cuddly it was and maybe, just maybe, grow to love that puppy as much as she herself loved it.

Little by little, Nikki saw her parents' attitudes soften. Even Jinx grew fond of the pups. And Nikki was delighted. Everything seemed to be working perfectly.

Yet, on a cloudy, cold November morning, Nikki's hopes were to be suddenly, completely shattered.

Having fed the puppies their morning chow, Nikki threw on her school clothes and hurried to the dining room with just time enough remaining to grab a bowl of cereal. Tyler, who had lately taken to walking both to

and from school with Nikki, waited for her in the hallway, where he sat by the phone table, scribbling a last-
minute math assignment.

Nikki smiled and said good morning to her parents. It
was not until after she'd poured the milk on her cereal
that she looked up long enough to take in the expression
on her father's face. Instantly, she feared in her heart
what was coming. She glanced quickly at her mother,
and found the same expression on her face.

"Nikki," her father began.

Swiftly, Nikki pushed her chair back. She straightened her dress and looked at her wristwatch.

"I've got to get going," she said. "I'm going to be late
for school."

If I can get away fast enough, she thought, this might
not happen. If I can just get outside before they have
time to say more . . .

Nikki's mother put a hand on her wrist, stopping her.
Mr. Savier uncomfortably adjusted his tie and his horn-
rimmed glasses. He cleared his throat.

"It's about the puppies," he said. "I'm sure you remember our agreement."

Oh yes, she remembered. No doubt about that. She
had just not imagined that such agreements could be
permanent—especially considering all she had done to
make things work, all the trouble she and Tyler had gone
to, all the love that had grown in her heart for the puppies. She turned her eyes desperately toward Tyler. His
pencil had stopped in midair and was poised uncertainly
above his paper. His eyes came up to Nikki's, but, for
once, they contained not the least light of reassurance.

Nikki turned back to her father. A hundred arguments rushed toward her tongue.

But before she could speak, her father raised a patient hand.

"You know what we agreed upon," he told her with quiet finality.

"But that was then," Nikki said. "That was seven weeks ago. Things are different now."

Mrs. Savier's fingers tightened slightly on Nikki's wrist. Her father merely shook his head.

The time had come, he told her. A deal was a deal. On Saturday he would take the puppies to the Animal Adoption Center. No ifs, ands, or buts about it.

10
Woe

After school, Nikki and Tyler trudged homeward as solemnly and slowly as mourners after a funeral. The wind blew coldly, lashing at Nikki's hair.

"They're heartless," Nikki said, bitterness sharp in her voice. "My parents are heartless."

Tyler nodded, out of sympathy for Nikki, rather than in agreement with her. He did not like to see the puppies go either, for he had become quite attached to them. But he was too practical in nature to overlook the good sense in Mr. Savier's decision. Tyler knew that Nikki had a heart the size of a watermelon, but he had not realized she would truly become so set on keeping all the puppies. He did not know what to say.

"How can they do this?" Nikki continued. "How can they turn their backs on an innocent bunch of harmless puppies and not think a thing about it?"

"Come on, now," Tyler argued gently, "I'm sure they'll all get good homes."

"You don't know that," Nikki retorted angrily. "*We* could have given them a good home, Tyler. We *have* given them a good home for the past seven weeks. But how do we know who'll take them from the adoption center?"

Tears forced themselves from Nikki's eyes and streamed down her cheeks. The wind made them feel like beads of ice. She walked swiftly onward, facing straight into the wind, her mouth set in a rigid frown, her eyes dark with woe.

"Your parents told you from the start that you couldn't keep the puppies," Tyler reminded her, becoming slightly exasperated. "There are just too many of them. Think about it, Nikki. What would you do with all those dogs?"

Nikki did not answer. She merely shook her head empathically and walked more swiftly yet, leaving Tyler behind.

"Don't cry, Nikki," Tyler pleaded, breathing hard as he tried to keep up with her, and feeling stupid for having taken her parents' side at such an inopportune moment. He reached up and thumped the top of his head, hoping he might knock some reassuring words loose from the depths of his brain. He could think of nothing at all to ease Nikki's pain, and he could not bear to see her so unhappy.

"You could have tried harder to convince your mother to take at least one puppy," Nikki accused, turning suddenly on Tyler.

"I told you, the manager of our building won't allow pets in the apartments. There's nothing I can do about that."

Abruptly, Nikki turned away from Tyler. She cut across the street and walked alone on the other side.

Feeling miserable and helpless, Tyler watched her from his side of the street. He felt he must do something, and do it quickly. But what? And why was he feeling this way? Nikki had been sad and disappointed before, and it had not hurt him as this was hurting. It was as if his friend's woeful feelings were invading his brain—like something out of a science fiction movie. In order to feel better himself, he must somehow make her feel better first.

And there seemed only one way of accomplishing that.

Slipping deeply into thought, Tyler crossed the street and walked some distance behind Nikki. From time to time, he closed his eyes, and he rubbed his forehead with his fingers, as Aladdin had once rubbed his magic lamp.

Little by little, something began to come to him. The thoughts in his head began to take on a shape, slowly but surely, like photographs developing in a chemical bath. At last, he was getting a grip on something. Tyler held on tight, and groped for more.

Reaching the corner of Maple, Nikki sat down on the grass of a vacant lot and put her face in her arms. Still lost in the whirl of his thoughts, Tyler wandered slowly to her side and sat down. He scratched his chin, pursed his lips, and gazed dreamily at the white, cloudy sky.

"It's just not fair," Nikki sobbed. "How can we let them go? Oh, Tyler, how can we do it?"

Tyler's eyes cleared as they came to rest on Nikki. Suddenly, a smile spread on his lips. He rose to his knees and clutched Nikki's shoulders.

"We're not going to let them go," he declared.

Nikki gaped at Tyler, blinking her eyes.

"What did you say?" she whispered.

"I said we're not going to let them go," Tyler firmly repeated. "Not if I can help it, Nikki. Now listen . . . I may have a plan. . . ."

11

The Plan

"Tyler, that is crazy," Nikki exclaimed.

She had listened to Tyler's plan and could not believe her ears. Yet, by all appearances, Tyler was perfectly serious.

"What's so crazy about it?" he challenged, not at all discouraged by Nikki's remark.

"A rent-a-puppy business? Tyler, get real."

"I am. Look, you want to keep the puppies, don't you?"

"Yes, but—"

"Just listen to me, Nikki," Tyler pressed on. "Your parents think you want to keep the puppies just because you like them, right? That seems unreasonable to them. But if we show how keeping the puppies could be a *lucrative* thing, then that's a whole new ball game. Do you see what I mean?"

"Lucrative?" Nikki repeated unsurely. "Chop a few syllables off your words, would you?"

"I mean," Tyler proceeded, carefully enunciating each word, "I mean, if we can demonstrate to your parents that we can take on complete responsibility for the puppies and that we can make the money that will feed them and pay for whatever else they need, then we're bound to gain an edge in pleading our case. Let's face it, adults love any idea where making money is involved."

Nikki shook her head and twisted her hair around and around her finger. It seemed to her that there were about a thousand and one holes in Tyler's scheme. The problem was, she couldn't see any one of them clearly, just yet.

"So you mean we'll rent out the puppies to people for a day, or a weekend, and with the money we make, we'll buy all the stuff they need?"

"Brilliant, isn't it," Tyler answered.

Ah ha, Nikki thought, there's a hole. A big one, too! "But Tyler . . . who is going to want to rent a puppy when he could just go out and buy one?"

But Tyler had an immediate response.

"A lot of people would! It's one thing to have fun with a puppy for a day or two, or even an hour or two, but another thing altogether to actually own the dog and have to feed it and clean up after it and buy a license for it and pay the vet bills. That's a lot of cash to spend, and a lot of trouble too, Nikki. Besides, there are many people, just like myself, who live in apartment buildings where dogs aren't allowed. But what's to keep them from renting a puppy for a day? Really, wake up, Nikki—this is the age of disposable commodities!"

Nikki couldn't help but smile at Tyler. His mind was so completely filled with the plan that the racing blood had overflowed and rushed to his cheeks. His bright, wide eyes looked almost wild.

"I do want to keep the pups," Nikki slowly agreed as new hope began to enter and fill her heart. "I guess anything is at least worth a try, isn't it?"

"You bet it is," Tyler answered, grasping Nikki's wrists and pulling her to her feet. "Come on, let's get to your place. We've got work to do before your parents get home!"

12
Business Partners

"Please, Dad, *please!*" Nikki pleaded in her most persuasive tone of voice. "Just give us a chance."

She was sitting in the whelping bed amid the band of puppies. The little dogs climbed about her lap, chewed on the hem of her sweater, and tussled with one another.

Tyler stood by the window, trying to maintain a calm, businesslike manner. This was not easy, for his heart was pounding and his teeth wanted to chatter. Tyler felt that his rent-a-puppy scheme was about the best idea he had ever come up with. All afternoon he had been calculating the fortune he and Nikki would make in the venture. The figures were astounding. Not only would they be able to keep the puppies—they would get rich in the bargain!

Mr. Savier slowly shook his head. In his hand was the sample advertisement Tyler had drawn up. For the second time, he read the paper:

PUPPIES ARE FUN!

Puppies can supply you with the love

44

and excitement you've been missing.
They are cuddly and playful, at home, in the park,
or wherever you choose.

Have you longed for the joy a tiny canine can bring,
yet felt you could not afford to own one?

WHY NOT RENT?

Now you can enjoy a puppy for a reasonable hourly,
daily, or weekly fee.
Special rates on Saturday and Sunday.

CONTACT:

Tyler G. Hubbs and/or Nicole S. Savier
at noon recess or after school
south end of playground by baseball backstop.

FRIENDLY SERVICE   **SATISFACTION GUARANTEED**

RENT-A-PUPPY, INC.

Mr. Savier grinned, tapping the advertisement with his index finger.

"It's really quite catchy," he commented.

"Henry!" Mrs. Savier exclaimed. "For goodness sake, the idea is absurd. It's impossible."

"Please," Nikki said, turning to her mother. "We'll keep the puppies right here in this room, and never let them out."

"Oh, and what happens when they bark and whine in the middle of the night?" Nikki's mother asked. "What do you plan to do—put gags on them?"

"Well, that shouldn't be a problem," Mr. Savier surmised. "I'm sure that Nikki plans to move her bed in here and sleep with the puppies."

"Huh?" Nikki said.

"It would be the only way to keep them quiet," her father continued. "I'm just wondering, now, how much I should charge you for rent. That is, if my study is going to be unavailable to me for some time to come."

"Rent?"

"Naturally. You and Tyler did figure on paying rent for the use of my room, didn't you?"

Nikki's mouth hung open like a broken screen door. She looked to Tyler for help.

"Uh, yes, certainly," Tyler said, nodding at Nikki's father. "I see your point. Until we can afford a larger, uh, *kennel* for our business, we'll have to rent this room. And, of course, Nikki will sleep with the puppies, to keep them quiet."

"But they don't sleep!" Nikki objected.

"Well, then, perhaps we shouldn't keep them after all," Mr. Savier suggested, looking down his nose and smiling triumphantly.

"Okay, all right, I'll sleep in here," Nikki quickly decided. "We'll move my bed in tonight."

Mr. Savier's smile wilted. He glanced at his wife. She too was frowning.

"Let us have a little conference," Mr. Savier said.

Nikki's mother and father left the room. They walked down the hallway to their own bedroom and closed the door behind them.

Nikki shifted to her knees in the box. The puppies

tumbled from her lap, rolled over one another like wobbly water balloons, then scrambled back to their feet, baying like grown beagles on a fox hunt.

"What do you think?" she said, nodding toward the hallway.

Tyler lifted a shoulder and raised an eyebrow. "At least they're discussing it," he remarked.

"By the way, thanks a load for volunteering me to sleep with these maniacs."

"You just don't understand sound business deals, Nikki," Tyler explained. "For now, we've got to give in to your parents' demands. Later, when we can demonstrate our success, we can negotiate for better terms."

Nikki rolled her eyes and smiled sourly. "I hope you know what you're talking about, because I sure don't."

"Quiet," Tyler said. "Here they come."

Mr. and Mrs. Savier reentered the room. For an unbearable minute, no one said a word.

At last, Mr. Savier sighed, scratched his chin with one hand, and slipped the other into the breast of his flannel shirt.

"Let me get this straight, once and for all," he said, standing very tall and formal as he fixed Nikki and Tyler in a long, hard gaze. "Everything these puppies need, you will provide—am I correct? Anything at all in the entire world that has to do with these little mongrels will be your and only your concern?"

"Yes, Dad," Nikki said. "Anything!"

Mr. Savier raised his eyebrows. He turned and looked at his wife. In unison, they grinned. It was a sly, conspiratorial sort of grin—the sort that people exchange when they are sharing a juicy secret. It made both Nikki and Tyler feel somewhat uncomfortable. They held their breaths, waiting for the unbearable silence to be broken.

"All right, then," Mr. Savier announced at last. "You've convinced us, Nikki."

"We can keep them?" Nikki said. Her knees trembled as she rose to her feet. Her head felt as light as a helium balloon.

Her father nodded, then smiled again in that mysterious way.

"One of us may regret this," he told her.

"It won't be me!" Nikki happily assured him, then quickly hid a wince as Hope's sharp little teeth clamped down on her ankle. "And I promise, Dad, you won't regret it either!"

13

Preparations

On Saturday morning the jubilant new business partners loaded the whelping bed into an old, rusty wagon and wheeled the puppies to the veterinarian. Nikki's parents had agreed to put the cost of the puppies' distemper shots on the family account, but made certain that she and Tyler understood they would be expected to pay the bill as soon as possible from the proceeds of the rent-a-puppy business.

"It's bound to be steep," Nikki said to Tyler as they walked side by side, taking turns at pulling on the handle of the wagon.

"No problem," Tyler confidently answered. "Before you know it, the money will be rolling into our pockets like balls on a pool table."

Arriving at the office, they parked the wagon outside the door. Nikki groaned as she lifted her end of the box. The puppies seemed to gaining weight by the hour.

"They feel more like cannonballs than puppies," Nikki said between her teeth.

"Next time we'll hire Arnold Schwarzenegger to help us," Tyler answered, fumbling to open the door with one hand while he held the box in the other.

Together, they stumbled to the receptionist's window.

"Please have a seat," the woman said, smiling into the box at the six furry little faces. "The doctor will be with you in a moment."

Dr. Williams had just finished with an enormous St. Bernard. He opened the office door and the huge dog came slinking out, eyes wide with terror.

"It's all over now," the dog's owner was saying as she patted his gigantic head. "No more shots until next year, Beany."

Tyler grinned at the dog's silly name. But Nikki's stomach had turned to Jell-O at the mention of shots. She was terrified of needles herself, and felt sorry for the big St. Bernard. At once, she realized there was no way she could bear to see the puppies receive their injections.

Dr. Williams walked across the waiting room and knelt in front of the box.

"That's quite a pack you have there," he said, lifting one end as Tyler lifted the other.

Nikki stayed glued to her chair.

"You go ahead, Tyler," she said shakily, trying to smile nonchalantly. "I'd rather stay here and, uh, read this magazine, if you don't mind." She snatched a copy of *Dog World* from the table beside her and buried her nose between the pages.

"Right." Tyler smiled knowingly at the doctor. "I'll take care of it, Nikki."

Waddling into the examination room, they hefted the unwieldy box onto the metal table. The doctor lifted Caddy from the midst of the unruly pack and began an examination.

"By the way, how much is this going to cost per pup?" Tyler asked.

"Twenty-three fifty," Dr. Williams told him.

Tyler's mouth snapped shut. His face went blank. Rapidly, he did some figuring in his head. The sum he came up with was frightful. It made his stomach sink like a rock in a pond.

"Something wrong?" Dr. Williams asked, raising a suspicious eyebrow as he returned Caddie to the box and lifted out Cubby.

"No, nothing," Tyler mumbled, tugging at his shirt collar. "It just feels a bit hot in here, that's all."

Feverishly, Tyler searched his mind for alternatives. Why not keep one puppy out, he thought? Subtract at least that much from the bill? What could it hurt? What was the chance that one puppy would get sick? One in a hundred? One in a thousand? Surely, the odds would be in the puppy's favor.

Dr. Williams refilled his syringe, then poked the needle into Cubby's rear end. The puppy yelped as its little feet tried to run on the slick metal table.

"Only five of the puppies need shots," Tyler suddenly blurted.

Reaching into the box, he pulled out Hope. This seemed a logical choice, for, after all, Hope had already been sick once and survived. Such puppies usually proved to be the strongest in the long run, didn't they?

"Are you sure?" Dr. Williams asked, narrowing his eyes.

"Yes, I'm sure," Tyler answered. "Of course I'm sure. This one has already had her shot," he lied.

Dr. Williams nodded his head and took the next puppy from the box. Tyler breathed with relief. A small cinder of guilt simmered at the back of his mind, but he did his best to squelch it. It's just superstition, Tyler told himself. And I'm not a superstitious person.

On the long walk home, Tyler and Nikki discussed their plans for the rent-a-puppy business. They figured what prices they should charge, how much of their income would have to be spent on dog food and vet care and squeaky toys, and how much they would be left with in profits. The latter detail was the one that had become the most exciting to Tyler. Bundles of green bills accumulated in his head as if he were a human bank vault.

"I wonder—" Nikki began, then paused. Nervous about something, she twisted her hair.

"What?" Tyler prompted.

"I wonder how I'm going to feel about letting the puppies go away with strangers, even for a day. How can we know they'll be safe? How can we know what kind of people we'll be dealing with? How . . ."

Tyler stopped walking. He placed a hand on Nikki's shoulder. Distracted by her new set of worries, Nikki closed her lips and gazed at Tyler. Tyler smiled widely, helpless to do anything else. Very often the sight of Nikki Savier's face simply made him want to smile.

"You really like these mutts, don't you," he said, and laughed. "Listen, Nikki, it'll be worth it. I know it will."

Reassured by Tyler's words, Nikki returned his smile.

"I know it will too," she said.

And she did her very best to believe the words.

14

Yes, We Deliver

On Monday at school, Tyler and Nikki pinned up Rent-a-Puppy posters at every available opportunity. Before the day was over, there was a poster on the wall of every hallway, on the bulletin board outside the office, and on the door of each of their homeroom classes.

At 3:20 sharp, the partners met by the fence at the south end of the playground. They did not have to wait for customers to arrive. Two were already waiting there for them.

"What's this all about?" said a large, roundish boy from one of the seventh-grade classes. He seemed to think the whole thing might be a joke.

"It's about renting a puppy," Tyler answered. "Are you interested?"

"No kidding?" the round boy said. "Where did you get the puppies?"

"They're ours," Nikki said. "We own them."

"How many ya got?"

"A hundred and fifty thousand," Nikki snapped. "Now do you want to rent one or not? If you don't, then move along. We've got business to do here."

"What's the matter with you?" Tyler whispered, catching Nikki's sleeve and yanking her aside.

Suddenly flustered, Nikki looked down and kicked at the grass with the toe of her shoe. What *is* the matter with me? she wondered.

"Customers, Tyler," she answered lamely, "you've got to know how to handle them."

Tyler frowned at Nikki, then returned his attention to the boy. He smiled his big, salesman's smile. "You can have a puppy for an hour, a day, a weekend, or whatever," he politely explained. "Here's a list of our prices."

"Maybe I will take one," the boy decided, looking at the list. "I'd have to ask my parents, though."

"Fine," Tyler said. "I'll be here for another half hour."

The boy nodded and smiled at Tyler. He began to walk away, then turned around.

"Oh, by the way, do you deliver?"

"Hey, we're not a pizza parlor," Nikki snapped again, seemingly unable to stop herself.

"Ahem!" Tyler quickly pushed Nikki away. "Yes, of course we deliver—as long as your house is within easy bike-riding distance."

"Good." The boy hurried away. "I think I'll get one," he called over his shoulder. "I'm almost sure I will."

"What do you mean 'we deliver'?" Nikki demanded, stepping in front of Tyler.

"Well, we're going to have to, aren't we? We can't expect everyone to come to your house for the puppies. What's the matter with you anyway? You were treating that kid like he was your worst enemy!"

"I guess you're right," Nikki admitted. "Maybe I'm just nervous. In fact, maybe you should handle all the up-front business, Tyler. I'll go home and take the puppies out to do their backyard business."

"Good enough," Tyler agreed. "Boy, you've got a lot to learn about polite business manners."

Nikki declined to answer. She merely waved and set off for home. She walked quickly, eager to get home to the puppies. She tried not to think, yet uneasiness fluttered in her stomach like butterflies. No matter how she tried to reason with herself, she just could not quite get used to the idea of farming out the puppies to total strangers. Deep down the idea made her nervous and fearful.

Back in the school yard, Tyler turned to his second customer. Two girls had also shown up, and each of them held a rent-a-puppy flier.

Beaming at the three potential renters, Tyler stepped jauntily forward and spread his arms wide.

"May I help you?" he said.

15

Success!

"We've got three probable rents for Saturday, and one certain rent for this evening!" Tyler joyously cried as he burst through the gate into the Savier's backyard.

Nikki barely heard Tyler's words. Her attention was riveted on the puppies as she dodged from one to another, trying to keep them within the bounds of the yard.

"Watch out for Albert Einstein, Jinx!" she gasped, out of breath. "He's getting away!"

"Listen to me, Nikki!" Tyler exclaimed, nearly tripping over Caddie as she raced between his legs. "Aren't you excited? I said we've got four rents already. And this is only Monday. By the time Friday comes around we'll have all six of the pups rented. And take a look at this!"

Tyler reached into his pocket and pulled out a handful of green bills. He spread the bills under Nikki's eyes like poker cards.

Nikki's face lit up at the sight of the money. Suddenly, she felt much better. Things really were working out, just as Tyler had said they would.

"You've rented one for tonight?" she asked.

"Right, I rented it to that first kid we talked to. He came back with the money just as I was about to leave. He wants us to deliver a puppy to his house. Any boy dog will do."

"So, which puppy are you going to deliver?" Nikki asked.

Tyler cast a thoughtful eye upon the puppies in the yard. He scratched his chin, pondering the question.

"Bluto," he decided. "And I'd better get going. The kid wants the puppy as soon as possible. I'll just run Bluto over to his house on your bike." As he spoke, Tyler walked toward the garage.

"But, Tyler—" Nikki began.

"Now, don't be selfish with your bike," Tyler scolded. "It's company transportation now, Nikki."

"But, Tyler, my bike has a flat."

Tyler stopped dead in his tracks. He stared at the bike leaning just inside the garage door against the wall. The front tire was as flat as a snake on a freeway. Tyler threw up his arms and groaned with frustration.

"Now you tell me!" he exclaimed.

"Well, you didn't ask until now."

"But the trip will take me twice as long on foot," Tyler complained. "We'll lose at least a half an hour's worth of rent money."

"What else can we do?" Nikki said.

"Wait a minute. What about Jinx's bike? Jinx has a bike, doesn't he?"

"Yes, but—"

"Bring it out here."

"But—"

"Bring it out!" Tyler commanded.

"All right, you asked for it," Nikki said. She disappeared into the garage for a moment, then returned with Jinx's bike. It was less than half the size of her own bike—more the size of a tricycle, really. There were two little jingling bells on the handlebars and a paste-on picture of Papa Smurf on the seat.

"That's a bike?" Tyler said.

"That's a bike," Nikki answered.

Tyler shook his head and let out a deep, defeated sigh. Gradually, however, his lips arched sharply upward in a smile of cunning.

"Okay, you're right," he said, clapping Nikki on the shoulder. "We'll have to use this bike until we can get your tire fixed. I'll just give you the address of this kid's house and you can—"

"Me!"

"Why, yes, of course, you," Tyler answered innocently. "I can't ride this thing, Nikki—that's obvious. I'm way too heavy. I'd break it for sure."

"Tyler G. Hubbs, if you think I'm going to get on that stupid little bike, you're out of your mind!"

"All right, then, Nikki," Tyler said with a great sigh, then hung his head in exaggerated despair. "I guess we'll just have to pass up this golden opportunity to rent our first puppy. Of course, that money sure would have come in handy. It sure would have helped toward paying our mounting bills, but—"

"Oh, all right, all right!" Nikki roughly grabbed the handlebars and straddled the tiny bike.

Tyler had to turn away and cover his mouth in order

to conceal his amusement. Nikki looked just like a circus clown on a unicycle.

"I must be crazy," she muttered bitterly.

"It's not all that small," Tyler fibbed. He bit his tongue in order to keep a straight face. "Really, you look just fine."

"Just shut up and give me the address," Nikki snapped.

Quickly, Tyler found a cardboard box in the garage. He returned to the yard, scooped up Bluto, and fit the wiggly puppy into the box, tucking down the flaps to keep him from escaping.

"Here's the address," he said, handing Nikki a scrap of paper as he placed the box into the bike's front basket.

Glumly, Nikki gazed at the darkly clouded sky.

"It's going to rain," she predicted.

Tyler looked up as well. He pursed his lips and scratched his chin.

"Just hurry over there and back," he advised in a knowledgeable tone of voice. "You'll beat the rain, I promise."

16

The Chase

Five minutes later, the dark clouds broke and the cold rain showered down.

"Jinx!" Tyler yelled, snatching Hope from the soggy grass and running to the porch as the rain pelted his head. "Jinx, help me get these puppies inside!"

He banged through the screen door, deposited the wet puppy on the clean linoleum, then hurried across the kitchen to close the door which led to the dining room and the rest of the house.

Jinx stood by the kitchen counter, dipping his hand into a jar of peanut butter.

"Aren't you going to help me?" Tyler said, swallowing distastefully as he watched Jinx suck gobs of the gooey peanut butter from his fingers.

"Nah," Jinx said, glancing out the window at the hissing sheet of rain. "It wouldn't be any fun."

"Look, Jinx, I'll pay you, okay?" Tyler fished deep into his pocket for the last of his coins. He had already had to pay Jinx for the use of his bike.

"Nah," Jinx repeated. "I got enough money already."

Grumbling, Tyler returned to the screen door. "Here, puppies," he called halfheartedly, then whistled between his teeth. "Come on pups."

The puppies paid him not the least bit of attention.

"Rats," Tyler cursed.

"You mean dogs," Jinx corrected through a mumbly mouthful of peanut butter. He giggled, drooling brown goo from the corners of his lips.

"Now listen closely, Jinx," Tyler warned, pointing a finger at the boy. "I'm going to round up these puppies and bring them into the kitchen. Whatever you do, don't let them out. Understand?"

"Mmm," Jinx answered, sucking in his cheeks and smacking his lips. "I got peanut bubber stuck to da woof of my mouf."

"You're breaking my heart," Tyler muttered as he stepped out the door.

In the yard, the puppies were having a wonderful time. They dashed about in crazy circles, sliding on the grass, rolling through mud puddles.

Tyler sighed, squared his shoulders, and forced himself into the drenching downpour.

"Hey there, Albert Einstein," he cooed as he approached. "Time to come in from the rain, old buddy."

But Albert Einstein, for reasons of his own, had no intention of coming in from the rain. The moment Tyler reached for him, Albert bounced away like a grasshopper.

"Oh, so that's the way you want it, huh?" Tyler said. "Well, two can play at that game, pal."

Crouching, Tyler moved stealthily forward. Albert

backed away in a series of playful leaps, his round eyes rolling with delight. Suddenly, Tyler let out a war cry and charged. He lost his footing on the slippery grass, stretched out in midair, and skidded, along with Albert Einstein, straight under the hedge and into old Mr. Gowper's backyard.

A moment later, Tyler reemerged from the hedge with mud on his face and Albert Einstein clutched solidly in one arm, with a hand on the scruff of his ragged, furry neck.

"Two down, three to go," Jinx gleefully encouraged as Tyler tossed the puppy into the kitchen.

"I'm going to get you, Jinx," Tyler hissed, almost as if he were letting off real steam, like a teapot. "You can count on it!"

Jinx giggled as he dipped his fat little hand into the jar of peanut butter.

Cubby and Caddie were the next to be captured. The two puppies were so constantly in each other's company that one might have thought they'd been born with their tails tied together. Tyler cornered the inseparable companions in the garden against the side of the house. He approached to within a couple of feet, then lurched forward, sinking inch-deep in the garden soil as he pinned the puppies against his chest.

"Ha, ha!" he cried jubilantly, spitting mud from his lips. "That's what I call killing two birds with one stone!"

Tyler slogged across the yard, stumbled up the porch steps, and sent the two pups tumbling across the kitchen floor to join the other prisoners within.

"Four down, one to go," he panted. "Ready or not, Sugar Baby, here I come!"

17

Deadline

Nikki arrived home on foot, wheeling Jinx's little bike at her side. It was not in any condition to be ridden. Not after the crash she'd had. The front wheel wiggled on its axle and emitted tortured squeaks and moans. The handlebars had been knocked askew when they hit the curbing. They stuck up in the air like elk antlers. Nikki's jeans were torn, her knees scraped. Reaching the garage, she removed the cardboard box from the basket, then fairly threw the little bike inside. She turned on her heel and walked stiffly to the house. On the porch, she began to wipe her feet on the doormat, then took a look at herself and threw up her arms in despair. She barged through the front door and slogged into the hallway. Rainwater dripped from the sleeves of her blouse, the cuffs of her pants, and the soggy cardboard box in her arms. Nikki sounded like a very leaky faucet, and looked like an angry creature from the deep.

"Where is he?" Nikki roared.

From the top of the stairway, both Jinx and Rox gaped down at her, certain that she had suddenly gone stark raving mad.

Nikki's eyes caught sight of the two. She stepped forward from her puddle of rainwater and began a new puddle at the bottom of the stairway.

"Where is he?" she repeated fiercely. "Where is Tyler?"

"Uh, I think he's busy," Jinx answered.

"Busy?" Nikki said. "Busy doing what?"

"Playing in the yard with the puppies," Jinx answered.

"Oh, playing, is he?" Nikki jeered, her dark eyes crackling with anger. "Playing, huh?" She pointed a finger at her brother. "Stay where you are, Jinx," she warned. "You don't want to see what's going to happen to him!"

Nikki's tennis shoes squeaked like two irritated mice as she plunged through the dining room and into the kitchen. Tyler had just come in through back door, the last outlaw puppy pinned securely in both arms.

The two faced each other from opposite ends of the kitchen, flushed and panting heavily.

"Tyler, prepare to die," Nikki declared, taking a threatening, extrasquishy step toward him.

"Now, just a minute, Nikki." Quickly, Tyler stepped backward, holding little Sugar Baby in front of himself like a shield. Rapidly he took in Nikki's condition. She looked as if she'd gone for a swim in her clothing. "Sure, you got a little wet out there," Tyler observed analytically, "but at least you got the job done, right? That's the important thing, now isn't it? Our first puppy has been rented and delivered."

"Oh yeah?" Nikki replied. "Guess again, buster."

She opened the top flaps of the box in her arms. Instantly, Bluto's floppy-eared head popped out, tongue wagging, eyes shining.

"Yap!" Bluto said.

Tyler stared in disbelief as Nikki lifted Bluto from the box and let the mushy cardboard fall to the floor. Thick droplets of muck rained from Bluto's fur. He looked as if he'd been dipped in a vat of milk chocolate.

"What on earth have you done to that dog?" Tyler demanded to know.

"I had an accident, okay? I crashed, okay? The kid wanted to rent a puppy, not a ball of barking mud!"

"*You* had an accident?" Tyler returned. "It looks more like Bluto had the accident."

"We both had the accident!" Nikki cried. "Just look at me!" She held her arms away from her body. The sleeves of her blouse dropped like the ill-fitting garment of a scarecrow.

"You do seem a tad moist," Tyler observed, grinning despite the dangerous look in Nikki's eyes.

"You're going to be smiling without teeth in two seconds," Nikki said, raising a white-knuckled fist.

"Well, look at me!" Tyler objected, backing up against the door and wondering how much Nikki would be deterred if he were to throw Sugar Baby at her.

For the first time, Nikki took notice of Tyler's sorry condition—his soaked and dilapidated clothing, the long, brown smudge down the front, his hair so wet and flat that it appeared to be painted on his head. Nikki's lips curved upward. She lowered her fist.

"The puppies decided to play a little game," Tyler explained.

"Catch us if you can?" Nikki guessed.

"You got it. I brought them in one by one." Tyler sounded like a frontier sheriff who had rounded up a band of notorious outlaws.

"So, where are they now?" Nikki asked, looking around. "Did you put them in the study?"

"No, I put them in the kit—chen." Tyler's voice stuck on the last word. He gazed past Nikki's shoulder at the open kitchen door. "Oh oh," he said.

Both realized, at the same instance, exactly what had happened.

"*Jinx!*" they bellowed in unison.

Small, running feet could be heard in the upstairs hallway, followed by the slam of a door.

"That does it!" Tyler said, starting toward the front of the house. "I warned him, I tell you, I *warned* him!"

"Wait a minute," Nikki said, grabbing Tyler's sleeve. "We'll massacre Jinx later, okay? Right now we've got"—she held up her arm and looked her wristwatch—"we've got exactly fifteen minutes to catch all the puppies and mop up the paw prints before my parents come home and massacre us!"

18

Cleanup Time

"You get the puppies," Nikki commanded. "I'll get the mop and the water."

At that moment, Cubby and Caddie came clattering into the dining room, took one look at Nikki and Tyler, then whirled and fled, barking and biting at each other's tails.

"Come to think of it, getting the puppies together is not going to be easy," Nikki unhappily observed. "We're never going to get this place cleaned up in time."

"Don't worry, I've got a plan," Tyler announced.

"Oh, a plan. Great! Another of Tyler Hubbs's wonderful plans. As if we don't have enough trouble already."

"Now, wait a minute," Tyler said, hurt by Nikki's attitude. After all, if it weren't for him, where would all these puppies be now? At the city animal shelter, that's where!

Nikki detected the hurt in Tyler's eyes, but she steeled herself and ignored it. She was cold, miserable, tired, and at any moment her parents would arrive home and she would be grounded for the rest of her life.

"All right, so what's your plan?" she demanded flatly.

Tyler smiled again, lifting his chin proudly.

"What is the one thing that will bring the puppies running to us?" he asked.

"Tyler, this is not a quiz show! If you've got a plan, spit it out!"

"The one thing that will bring the puppies running," Tyler continued, unruffled, "is the sound of food being poured into a bowl."

Nikki raised one thoughtful eyebrow, pleased despite her contrary mood. "Good plan," she agreed. "I'll go up to the study and get the Kibbles."

"No time for that," Tyler said. "Let's just use Roxie's food."

"You know what my parents said about that," Nikki objected. "We're only supposed to feed the puppies the dog food we buy ourselves."

"Yes, but this is an emergency," Tyler reminded her.

Nikki hesitated only a second. Glancing once more at her watch, then at the mess in the kitchen and dining room, she quickly cast her objections aside and hurried to the cupboard under the sink to pull out Roxie's gigantic bag of Gravy Train. "This thing weighs a ton," she complained, grunting as she lifted the bag.

"Just get it over here and get pouring," Tyler said.

"Who do I look like? Hercules?"

"Oh, never mind!" Tyler shouldered past Nikki, lifted the bag, and struggled back toward the big plastic bowl.

In the meantime, Roxanne, possessing a nose and ears as good as any beagle's, came trotting down the stairs and into the kitchen, her tongue wagging hungrily. She went straight to her bowl, fully prepared to pig out.

"Rox, go away," Nikki scolded. "You'll ruin everything. It's not time for your dinner."

She poked Rox with the business end of the mop. Startled, Rox jumped away from the bowl. She stared at Nikki, utter indignation smoldering in her eyes.

"Go on, now, I mean it!" Nikki said, threatening again with the mop handle.

Reluctantly, Rox retreated, glancing sorrowfully over her shoulder.

"Okay, Tyler, she's gone," Nikki said. "We still have ten minutes. Pour! Pour!"

Tyler tipped the enormous bag and the Gravy Train clattered noisily into the bowl. Within seconds the six puppies came running from every corner of the house and crowded to the plastic dish like ravenous piglets.

"See what I told you," Tyler remarked, beaming. "Instant puppies, guaranteed!"

19

Attack

Nikki and Tyler stood back as the puppies pushed and shoved each other around the rim of the bowl. Their six pink mouths worked steadily at the crunchy food like garbage compactors.

Tyler shook his head and nudged Nikki with his elbow. Nikki giggled, but then remembered that there was work to be done, and only minutes in which to do it.

She turned toward the sink, then stopped abruptly. Out of the corner of her eye she had caught sight of Roxanne. She was under the dining room table, and she was standing in a tense, flexed manner—like a fat stone cocked back in the pocket of a slingshot.

"Look out!" Nikki screamed.

Tyler turned just in time to see Rox blast like a cannonball from under the table, ears flying, lips raised above her teeth, bloodshot eyes fixed fiercely upon the puppies.

Before Tyler or Nikki could move, Rox launched herself into the unwary passel of puppies and sent them toppling like six upended bowling pins.

"Rox—stop!" Nikki cried.

But Rox was a dog possessed. She could see nothing but the six treacherous pups, gobbling *her* food, eating from *her* bowl!

The green bowl went twirling after the fleeing puppies, ejecting bits of Gravy Train in every direction. Rox shot through the chunky, brown rain like a guided missile, fixing her sights on one puppy.

Caddie, the unlucky target, tried desperately to get out of the way. Instead, she lost her footing and tumbled straight into the jaws of the monster, her mother. Rox lowered her snout, caught Caddie under the stomach, and flipped her high in the air.

Diving to break the puppy's fall, Tyler skidded over the rolling chunks of dog food and directly into the open broom closet, where he rammed his head into neatly stacked bottles of floor wax and window cleaner. Caddie, too terrified to be thankful, mindlessly bit Tyler's thumb.

"Roxanne, stop this! I mean it!" Nikki shouted.

She grabbed for Roxie's tail, but Rox swiftly dodged the attempt, reversed her field as nimbly as a great athlete, and charged after the remaining five puppies as they made an attempt to escape to the dining room.

Clang-briiing! The telephone crashed to the floor. So did a glass vase filled with flowers and a cup containing about half a million pencils.

The puppies bolted frantically toward the center of the room, huddling close together like a horde of routed soldiers. They stumbled, rolled, somersaulted on the scattered pencils.

On top of them in half a second, Rox descended like a

giant predator spider—a swift, stout-legged, canine tarantula! She batted the puppies off their feet, using her snout as a cudgel, and scooped them back with her front paws whenever they threatened to slip free.

Determined not the miss out on the action, Jinx came pounding down the stairs. As he entered the dining room, his feet hit the pencils, went out from under him, and Jinx thumped to the floor, bouncing once on his rear end. "Get 'em, Rox!" he screeched with delight.

Pitching herself forward, Nikki caught hold of Roxie's shoulders. At the same time, Tyler slid behind her and captured her tail. Both hollered at the top of their lungs for Rox to cease her attack.

And neither of them heard Nikki's parents come in the front door.

Locked in combat with Rox, they remained completely unaware as Mr. Savier walked into the dining room and stood directly behind them.

Until he spoke, that is. Then they heard him very well.

"What in blazes is going on here?" he boomed.

Tyler, Nikki, Rox, the puppies—all froze as if the voice had been a subzero, blizzard-force wind. Slowly, Nikki and Tyler let go of Roxie's fur. Rox released the puppies and timidly wagged her tail, sweeping pencils to and fro. She craned her neck in her master's direction, smiling as warmly as she could manage under the circumstances, then slunk away in search of safety.

Mr. Savier's hands were on his hips. His face was faintly purple and his cheeks strangely puffy, as if they were about to burst like two overinflated party balloons.

In the deep blue of his eyes raged an approaching storm. Behind him, in the archway to the hall, stood Mrs. Savier. She gazed with humorless disbelief upon the battlefield Rox and the puppies had made of her house.

"Dad, just give us a chance to explain," Nikki began.

"Silence!" her father commanded.

Nikki watched as he struggled with his boiling emotions. Very quietly, Tyler began to pick up the pencils. He handled them with exaggerated care, as if they were injured birds.

For an agonizing half minute, the only sound was that of Jinx giggling from under the table, where he and Rox had chosen to hide.

At last, Mr. Savier's cheeks deflated. He cleared his throat, straightened his tie, and slipped his right hand into the front of his suit coat.

"Clean it up," he ordered, in a whisper of carefully concealed fury. "I'll give the two of you five minutes to clean this mess—and you'd better get every last bit of it!"

20

Business Conference

It took them not five minutes, but more than an hour to clean up the paw prints and the broken glass, the pencils and the flowers and the widely scattered dog food. Exhausted and demoralized, they retreated to the study, where the puppies, having been finally corralled, lay knit together in their box. Nikki threw herself, stomach first, on the bed. Tyler slumped into a chair.

"I don't know," he lamented through a long, tired breath. "I just don't know. . . ."

"You don't know what?" Nikki asked, turning on her side to face him.

Tyler opened his mouth to answer, but then stopped himself. He was about to say that they might be in over their heads—that possibly, just possibly, he had underestimated the hazards and pitfalls of running a business—especially where six uncontrollable puppies were involved. But then his eyes alighted on Nikki's face, and Tyler knew he could not speak, for Nikki's eyes were on the puppies and were filled with the same ardent love she had felt for them from the beginning, despite today's disaster. Tyler turned his eyes to the puppies also, and found that he had to smile. There they lay, as quiet and harmless as stuffed teddy bears.

"Tyler?" Nikki said, propping herself up on one elbow. "What were you going to say?"

"Nothing," Tyler answered. "Never mind."

One of the puppies sneezed, distracting Nikki's attention from Tyler's hesitant reply. Nikki swung her legs off the bed and leaned toward the box.

"Which one is sneezing?" she said.

"I think it's Hope," Tyler answered.

Nikki rose and walked quietly to the box. She knelt and looked at Hope's sleepy face.

"Look how her poor nose is running," she said.

"Maybe she caught a cold out in the yard today," Tyler suggested.

"Dogs don't catch colds, do they?"

"Oh, I'm not sure." Tyler shrugged.

"Well, what do you think is wrong?"

"I don't know. Maybe she's just a naturally snotty-nosed dog."

Nikki returned to the bed, too tired to come up with a reply.

"You know," Tyler remarked after some moments of silence, "I thought your dad might terminate the rent-a-puppy business after what happened this afternoon."

"So did I," Nikki agreed in a perplexed tone of voice. Her eyes narrowed with thought. "Maybe he's waiting for us to fail on our own," she added.

"But we're not going to, are we?" Tyler said, sitting up straight in his chair. He did not like to see Nikki becoming gloomy over their prospects. And he did not like to admit failure himself. After all, he had promised Nikki that his plan would work. What would she think of him if the whole thing were to come crashing down like a house of cards?

"Look," Tyler continued, "I realize that what happened this afternoon was bad for business, but we can't let that stop us. No business venture was ever without its setbacks. Just look at the Wright brothers, for instance. Their first airplane didn't fly."

Nikki couldn't help but smile at Tyler's earnestness.

"I don't think the puppies will ever fly," she teased.

"You know what I mean," Tyler answered humorlessly. "We've still got two rents for the weekend. By the time it gets here, we could have all six rented."

"Maybe," Nikki allowed through a yawn, lying back on the bed.

Tyler picked up a pad of paper and began to deduct the costs of the items Rox and the puppies had broken from the nonexistent fund pool of the rent-a-puppy business. He mumbled as he wrote.

"Don't forget the bottles you wasted with your head when you slid into the broom closet," Nikki reminded him. "My mom says we have to pay for them."

"Lucky thing I didn't break my skull," Tyler answered sullenly.

"Yeah, then you'd have to pay for that too."

"Very funny."

Nikki giggled.

"By the way," she said, "the kid who rented Bluto wants his money back."

"I figured."

Nikki sat up on the bed, smiling at something. "Did you know that puppies can swim without taking lessons?" she asked.

"Huh?" Tyler glanced up from his computations.

"Yeah. When I crashed the bike, Bluto blasted off from the front basket like the space shuttle and landed in a construction ditch filled with muddy water. He swam right out of there like an Olympic champion."

"Good, that means we won't have to pay for any lessons at the YMCA," Tyler observed.

At this, Nikki began to laugh. Soon Tyler was laughing also, and they both laughed so hard that tears tumbled down their cheeks. Nikki rolled off the bed, clunking to the floor. She held her sides while Tyler gasped for air. At last, when they were able to stop, they were more exhausted than ever.

"This whole day has made us silly," Tyler said, slowly regaining his composure.

Nikki nodded in agreement, brushing her wild hair from her eyes.

"Tomorrow," she said. "Tomorrow will be a better day."

"That's a safe prediction," Tyler added. "How could it be any worse?"

21

Messages

Tomorrow was a better day. So were the next and the next. And Saturday was shaping up to be the best day of all.

Just as Tyler had predicted, all six puppies had been rented. By ten o'clock in the morning each had been delivered into the arms of its renter, and Tyler's pocket was full of paper money.

He and Nikki sat on the front steps by the sidewalk. It was an uncommonly mild day for mid-November. The sky was clear except for a few puffy clouds in the east— perfect puppy-renting weather. Tyler counted the money, bill after bill. He loved the crisp feel of the bills, and the rich smell they left on his fingertips.

"It's kind of weird having all the puppies gone," Nikki commented. "Isn't it, Tyler?"

"It's wonderful," Tyler mumbled absentmindedly, counting the money for a second time.

Nikki frowned at the intense expression on Tyler's face.

"I'm kind of worried about Hope," she pressed, leaning close to Tyler, bumping his knee with hers. "She was sneezing again this morning."

"Hmm?" Tyler said, glancing up from his riches. His eyes met Nikki's and instantly he saw her concern. "Oh, sneezing," he said, folding the money and returning it to his pocket. "Maybe she's allergic to something," he suggested.

Nikki nodded, hoping that Tyler was right.

"I suppose she'll be okay," she said.

"Of course she'll be okay," Tyler answered confidently. "They'll all be okay. Why wouldn't they be? No one is going to be shooting them out of cannons, are they?"

"I guess not," Nikki said, and smiled.

"Lighten up," Tyler advised. "Trust me—things couldn't be better, Nikki."

Again Nikki nodded, and she smiled more widely. Sitting so close to Tyler, it was easy to breathe in his confidence and make it her own.

For the remainder of the morning and most of the afternoon, Tyler and Nikki went about their own pursuits. Tyler washed his mother's car, then read a copy of *Fortune* magazine from cover to cover. Nikki walked to the supermarket and bought a couple of squeaky toys for the puppies, then stopped by a girlfriend's house on the way home. For once, neither Nikki nor Tyler had a care in the world. They had been caught up in the puppies for so long, that each had almost forgotten to live lives of their own.

It was four o'clock when they met again at Nikki's house. Mrs. Savier was waiting for them at the door. She frowned as she handed Nikki a piece of paper from a notepad.

The paper said:

Telephone Messages for RAP, Inc.
11:00 A.M.—Mrs. Brown, rent disagreement.
11:45—Mrs. Gotter, broken property.
1:10 P.M.—Mr. Allington, possible legal action.
3:10—Alice Coventry, bitten on nose.

As she read the list, Nikki's face turned white. Tyler's forehead broke out in a cold sweat.

"What are we doing to do?" Nikki said.

"Now, don't get excited," Tyler advised, quickly pulling himself together. "Let's just telephone these people and see what has happened."

"But we're going to owe about a million bucks by the time this day is over!"

"Don't jump to conclusions, Nikki. Always maintain a professional attitude."

Tyler carried the telephone to the study and dialed the first number.

"Mrs. Brown says Bluto is not potty trained," he reported after hanging up. "She says she wants half her money back."

Nikki groaned. Tyler dialed again.

"Mrs. Gotter wants *all* of her money back, plus a twenty-five percent damage fee for the leg of a coffee table which she claims Caddie ate."

"Ate?" Nikki protested. "That's impossible. She's got

to be exaggerating. Caddie's only a puppy—not a great white shark!"

Tyler shrugged a shoulder and dialed the next number on the list.

"Mr. Allington accuses us of fraudulent advertising," he reported. "He says we advertised puppies, but delivered lethal weapons. Apparently we have some more broken property to pay for."

"Is he going to take us to court?" Nikki asked. She had a great fear of being branded a criminal and dragged into court. She could clearly imagine being rudely badgered by a judge on TV—her shame exposed to millions of viewers.

"I think we can bargain our way out of a court appearance," Tyler assured her.

Lastly, Tyler telephoned Alicia Coventry, the girl with the bitten nose. Alicia couldn't come to the phone, her mother informed Tyler. She was busy holding a washcloth to her injured nose.

"Oh, I'm sorry," Tyler said. "But I am glad to hear that it's still there."

"What is?"

"Your daughter's nose. I mean, uh, is it very badly bitten, ma'am? I suppose we could refund your rent money."

"You certainly could," Alicia's mother answered haughtily. "And you certainly will!"

Glumly, Tyler returned the receiver to its cradle. He looked at Nikki. She was holding her head as if it were about to fall off her shoulders.

Suddenly the telephone rang. Unnerved, Nikki and

Tyler jumped back. They stared at the phone as it rang a second time, then a third.

"Don't answer it," Nikki advised. "It's more bad news, I just know it is."

"Don't be silly," Tyler said. "It's probably not even for us."

The phone rang again and again.

"Oh, for heaven's sake!" Tyler snatched up the receiver. "Hello!" he barked. "Savier residence, Tyler Hubbs speaking."

Nikki looked on as Tyler's face turned red, then white, then red again. She could not tell what the conversation was about from Tyler's vague "ums" and "ohs," but she could tell that the news was bad, maybe the worst news they'd had all day.

"All right . . . yes . . . we'll see what we can do," Tyler concluded, then slowly hung up the receiver. He looked at Nikki, but did not speak. He seemed stunned, unable to form words.

"What is it?" Nikki asked, gripping his knee. "What happened? Is it one of the puppies?"

"Yes," Tyler said. "It's Hope."

"Hope? What about Hope?"

"Gary Smith and his dad had her up in Skyler Park. They were having a picnic up there. Hope wandered off about two o'clock. They haven't seen her since." Tyler swallowed, then cleared his throat. "She's lost, Nikki," he finished. "Hope is lost."

22

Lost Dog

Skyler Park was the nearest thing that could be found in the city to a patch of tangled, untracked wilderness. It was a very large park—one big, rolling hill covered with pines and firs. The ground was choked with twisting vines, jumbles of sticker bushes, and large patches of green, waxy ivy.

Nikki and Tyler arrived at the park out of breath, having run all the way. They found Gary Smith and his father near the picnic tables. In a shaky voice, Gary explained that he had been playing with Hope, had left her a moment to roast a second wiener, and the next thing he knew, Hope was gone.

"We looked high and low," Gary's father assured Tyler. "The puppy has simply disappeared from the face of the earth."

"We've got to find her," Nikki said. She was trying to remain calm, but her heart was trembling like a leaf in a storm.

"We'll find her," Tyler answered coolly, maintaining a calm, confident attitude for Nikki's sake, even as his stomach was turning worried somersaults. "Let's all split up. Nikki, you go up the hill a ways. I'll check that ravine over there."

The four searchers separated. Hope's name was echoed back and forth as Tyler, Nikki, Gary Smith, and his father drew farther and farther apart.

"Hope?" Nikki called. "Please, Hope . . . where are you?"

A half hour passed. Still no luck. The sun dropped low on the western horizon, casting a gloomy orange veil about the tall fir trees.

Tyler hiked down into the ravine, following thin trails which cut between the snaggled undergrowth. He peered behind every tree, under every bush.

Where could she have gone? he wondered. Maybe she was sick, as Nikki had suggested earlier. Maybe Hope had gone off to . . . to . . .

Tyler did not want to think about it. Silently, he cursed himself for having denied Hope her shots. If Hope should be sick, the fault would be entirely his own. How could he explain his actions to Nikki? He could never, never hope to be forgiven; and he would lose her friendship forever. The thought made his trembling stomach ache with emptiness.

"Hope?" Tyler called loudly, his voice breaking. "Hope, where are you?"

Suddenly, Tyler froze in his tracks. He was certain he had heard something—a very weak bark. Again, he called out, then held his breath. He closed his eyes and listened.

There it was again! Definitely a bark. It came from above, back up the ravine.

Tyler scrambled up the trail, shouting Hope's name as he went. Another bark reached his ears. He was getting nearer to the sound. Ten more yards. Five yards. He must be right on top of it now.

Sweat flowed from Tyler's forehead as he threw himself on his hands and knees and frantically searched the dim tunnels which twisted and crisscrossed beneath the brambles. He thrust his hands into the tangle of leaves and stickers, oblivious of the scratches he received. He crawled frantically forward into the hip-high jungle.

At last, he found her. Hope lay tucked in a nest of fallen leaves, almost totally hidden from sight. She lay on her side, trembling, her legs curled close to her body.

Tyler screamed with joy, snatching the puppy into his hands and pressing her to his chest.

"Nikki!" he shouted. "Nikki—I found her!"

From far away came Nikki's shouts of elation. Tyler could hear her calling to Gary and his father.

"You crazy dog," Tyler scolded, holding Hope in front of his face. "Just what do you think you're doing?"

At once, Tyler's gladness turned to despair as he took a close look at Hope's eyes. They were foggy and seemed not to see him. Sickly mucus dripped from her nose. Her sides heaved in and out, in and out, as if she couldn't catch her breath, even in all this crisp, open air.

"Oh no," Tyler said. A shiver of fear darted up his spine. "Oh no, oh no."

Cradling the puppy in his arms, Tyler ran headlong toward the top of the ravine. Illogically, he felt that if only he could run fast enough, get Hope to the top of the hill quickly enough, everything would be all right. Magically, Hope would be well.

Nikki came on a run to meet Tyler, as did Gary and his father. Bright smiles of relief beamed on their faces. But their smiles wilted like plucked rose petals the moment they came close enough to see Tyler's anguished expression.

"What's wrong with her?" Nikki asked, cupping Hope's snout gently in her palms. "What happened?"

"I'm afraid she's sick," Tyler answered hollowly.

"Sick?" Nikki said, sounding as if the word had no meaning in the English language. She stared at Tyler, waiting for an explanation.

"I think it's distemper," Tyler admitted. It hurt him to say the word. It felt like a knife twisting in his heart. What have I done? What have I done? Tyler's mind echoed over and over.

"But how?" Nikki said. "She had her shot, just like all the others."

Tyler hung his head. His Adam's apple moved up and down, wanting to choke off the words Tyler knew he must say.

"Nikki . . . Hope didn't have the shot," he answered. He forced himself onward. "I figured since she had already been sick once, that she wouldn't get sick again. I didn't think she would need the shot." Tyler gulped. He put one hand to his throat. The part to come was almost too terrible to utter. "I was trying to save us some money," he finished in a tortured whisper.

Nikki's hand rose slowly to her lips. Her eyes widened with horror as she stood stiffly in place, staring, dumbstruck, at Tyler.

"I'm sorry," Tyler hopelessly rasped, knowing that his words could mean nothing to Nikki. "Nikki, I'm sorry. I'm really sorry."

"I think we'd better get this puppy to a veterinarian," Mr. Smith suggested quietly, looking sympathetically from Nikki to Tyler. "Come on, my car is in the lot. I'll take you there myself."

23

Hope-less

Nikki ran all the way home from Dr. Williams's office, hardly able to see through her tears as the sidewalk jogged up and down beneath her feet. Slamming through the front door, she rushed to the study, threw herself on the bed, and buried her face in her arms. Her shoulders shook as she let out her sobs.

She could not believe what had happened. How could Tyler have done this thing, knowing that Hope might get sick? Knowing that Hope might die.

In her mind's eye, Nikki saw herself standing in the veterinarian's office, desperately looking on as he lifted and examined Hope's weak, limp body, shaking his head all the while. She could still hear Hope's small wheezes and whimperings.

"There's not much I can do," Dr. Williams had said. "I'm afraid my best advice would be to have the puppy put to sleep."

Nikki winced, as surely as if his words had been nails.

"How could you!" she'd finally howled at Tyler, her fists clenched, tears stinging in her eyes. "How could you! How could you!"

Tyler had opened his mouth to speak. That was when Nikki bolted from the office. She could not bear to hear another word.

Later, at home, ever present in Nikki's mind, was the image of Hope. The little pup had looked so miserable, only half-alive. How could it have happened so suddenly? Or had she herself been blind to the truth—thinking too much about the money she and Tyler were making, and of her own desire to keep the puppies, no matter what? Thinking not of Hope, nor of any of the puppies, but only of herself. Oh, if only she could bring Hope back—if only she could make Hope well again—she would do anything, she would give all the pups away this minute! If only . . .

It's my fault, Nikki decided, weeping into her pillow. What has happened to Hope is all my fault.

The door creaked open and Rox padded quietly into the room, followed by Jinx. They sat down on the floor next to the bed. Rox and Jinx were always together these days, for Jinx had learned a lesson of his own during the past few weeks. He understood, now, that Rox would not harm anyone on purpose. He'd seen what a good mother she was, just like his own mother, and he'd come to feel as safe with Rox as one of her own pups.

Roxanne whimpered twice, then placed her snout on the edge of the mattress. She touched her nose to Nikki's and her long pink tongue rolled out to lick a tear.

"Oh, Rox," Nikki said, hugging her neck. "You knew what was best all along, didn't you? You knew that puppies need to grow up, go out on their own, fend for themselves, find people to live with, a family of their own. It's the natural way, isn't it?" Gently, she scratched Roxie's ears, feeling as if the dog understood every word she had spoken. "I wish you could talk," she said. "You could have told me what would happen from the start."

"I had to grow up too," Jinx said. He began to cry, simply because his sister was crying. She was the happiest person he knew, and her sudden unhappiness seemed terribly out of place—as if something had gone wrong in the functioning of the entire world. "You used to take care of me all the time," Jinx sniffled.

Nikki placed her hand upon her brother's head. She tried to smile, but could not.

There was a light tapping on the door. Nikki's mother and father came in. Together they sat down on the foot of the bed.

"Nikki . . . I'm sorry," her father said, reaching over to brush a hand through her hair. "This thing with the puppies . . . it never should've gone this far." He shook his head and sighed deeply, then went on. "When you wanted so badly to keep the pups, despite our advice, your mother and I decided that . . . well, we decided that we'd let you go ahead and try, just so you'd see for yourself how impossible it would turn out to be. We wanted you to learn a certain lesson. But we never imagined something like this would happen, Nikki. We never wanted any of the pups to be sick. It's my fault, really. It was my idea to allow you and Tyler to go ahead with your plan."

Nikki shook her head. She wanted to tell her father that she had known this all along. She wanted to tell him that it was not his fault. But she could not speak. She knew that if she were to try, only anguished sobs would come forth.

Mr. Savier sighed and put his chin in his hand.

"Tell you what," he said, "I'll take care of your customers tonight when they bring the puppies home. Okay, Nikki?"

"Okay," Nikki managed hoarsely. "Thank you, Dad."

"By the way," Nikki's mother added softly, "Tyler called about ten minutes ago. I told him you'll call him back when you felt a little better."

"No," Nikki said. "I won't call him back. I'm never talking to Tyler again."

Without another word, her parents left the room, along with Jinx and Rox. Nikki was left alone with her thoughts. Alone with the terrible sadness and regret that burned in her heart like searing flames.

24

A Talk with Her Father

For the next four days Nikki lived like a sleepwalker. At school she wandered the halls between classes, hardly aware of where she was going. She stared straight ahead and spoke not a word. She sat through her classes without hearing her teachers' words. Constantly, there was a throbbing ache in her stomach, an emptiness as big as all outer space. And she tried not to think of Hope. She tried not to think of any of the puppies. They seemed so lonely all of a sudden—always together in a pack, yet missing the special attention that single pets receive. They missed Hope too. Nikki could tell. From time to time they seemed to know what had happened.

Nikki did not see Tyler at school, and she did not care to. Had she seen him, she would have run and found a place to hide, for she could not bear to face him again—to face the sadness that had come between them.

On Sunday, Tyler called twice on the phone, once in the morning and again in the afternoon. Both times, Nikki refused to answer. Nor did she return his calls.

On Monday when she walked in the door after school,

the phone was ringing. But Nikki knew who it was. She let the phone ring until it stopped.

At last, Wednesday afternoon arrived and school was let out for Thanksgiving vacation. Nikki walked home alone, as she had done all week, and went directly to the study, back to the puppies, all in need of her love.

Yet, as Nikki sat with the pups on the floor, letting them play on her lap and tug at her shoelaces, she knew in her heart that she could not give them the love they deserved. She was only one person, trying to do the impossible. She was one person, trying to divide her heart in five pieces. And it hurt. It could not go on this way.

That night Nikki found her father in his easy chair reading another book about Napoléon Bonaparte and making notes on a yellow pad as he read. It was late, but Nikki had known that he would still be up. She walked across the room and sat down by his feet. Puffing on his pipe, he looked at her through big, perfect rings of maple-scented smoke.

"How's my girl?" he asked.

Nikki hesitated, preparing herself to say what she knew she must.

"Dad . . . I want to find new homes for the puppies."

Her father sat forward and placed a hand on her shoulder.

"I talked to a few kids at school today," Nikki pressed on. "A couple of them said they'd like to have a puppy. They're going to ask their parents if it's okay."

"That sounds encouraging," Mr. Savier commented.

"It would have been best from the start," Nikki said.

"I know that now. I see how lonely the puppies are. And Roxie . . . well, Roxie's sad too. Everyone is sad."

"Rox is just used to being top dog," Mr. Savier explained.

"I know, but it's more than that, Dad. I believe Rox knew from the beginning that the puppies couldn't stay. Remember when she weaned them? She left the box, even though they were all crying for her to come back. It just about broke my heart at the time, and I even tried to force Rox to go back to the box. But she wouldn't do it. She knew what was best."

"Sometimes dogs have more common sense than people," Nikki's father agreed. "They sure do things in simpler ways."

Yes, Nikki thought, dogs do have simple ways of doing things. Ways that work. Ways that rely on instincts alone.

"Do you think we can find homes for the puppies," Nikki asked. "All six—" She stopped herself. Hope's face came to her mind. The sadness came back like a heavy weight in her chest. "All five of them, I mean?" she finished.

"I don't see why not. All considered, they'd make wonderful pets. One per person, that is."

Nikki nodded and swallowed a lump in her throat. Her father leaned forward and looked closely at her face. His eyes seemed especially blue and kind.

"Have you talked yet to Tyler?" he asked.

Nikki shook her head.

"Honestly, Nikki, don't you think it's time you talked to him?"

"Why? Why should I?" Nikki recoiled automatically.

"If it hadn't been for Tyler, none of this would have happened. None of this trouble would have ever begun, and Hope wouldn't have gotten sick. She wouldn't have—"

"Now, wait a minute," Mr. Savier gently interrupted. "Whose idea was it in the first place to keep all the puppies? Do you remember, Nikki?"

Nikki admitted the truth in a whisper.

"Listen to me, Nikki," her father continued. "Why do you think Tyler came up with this rent-a-puppy scheme of his?"

"Why? Well, to make money."

"No, I don't think that's it. That was one result of the plan, sure. But why did he rack his brains to come up with the idea to begin with? He certainly went to a lot of trouble. Was it because he wanted to keep all those puppies as much as you did?"

Nikki considered her father's question. Tyler liked the puppies, of course. She knew that. But he was also a very practical sort of person. If it were not for Nikki herself, would he ever have concocted such a difficult scheme? Nikki opened her mouth to speak but then shook her head slowly. She did not know the answer. Confusion swam in her eyes as she pondered.

Mr. Savier smiled. The wrinkles at the corners of his eyes turned upward.

"Tyler did this for you, Nikki," he said, as if it were the simplest conclusion in the world, the answer to two plus two. "He did it for one reason only, Nikki. He simply wanted to make you happy."

*   *   *

For a long time Nikki lay in her bed without sleeping. The puppies were curled about her feet on the blanket. They had learned to claw their way to the top of the mattress, like marines climbing a rope ladder. In the past, Nikki might have put them back in their box. But tonight she did not mind their presence. Soon they would be leaving her. At last, she was ready to face that thought. But until they were gone, she would let them get just as close to her as they wanted.

Nikki's head was filled with the events of the past few weeks, and as always, the memory of Hope throbbed like a fresh wound. But what she thought about most of all, just now, was what her father had said about Tyler.

Tyler did it for you.

Yes, it was simple. Nikki saw, now, how very simple it had been. Tyler had tried to build a business on *her* unrealistic hopes—a business built not on good sense, but on emotions and friendship. As she pondered this, Nikki found herself feeling something new for Tyler—something she'd never felt before, for anyone. It occurred to her, suddenly, that she had been very cruel over the past few days. She had thought only of herself, of her own loss, and nothing of what Tyler might be feeling. Now she thought of him, and an odd sort of ache came to her heart. Suddenly, she missed him very much.

She would make it up to him, Nikki decided at once. Tomorrow was Thanksgiving—what better day on which to mend a friendship?

"He did it for me," Nikki whispered in the darkness.

And soon after, she was fast asleep.

25

Thanksgiving Morning

Immediately after breakfast, Nikki ran all the way to Tyler's apartment building. She paused briefly on the first flight of steps, thinking about Hope and feeling bad inside. But she couldn't change what had happened. She would just have to go on from here, and so would Tyler. At least they could go on together—if it wasn't too late for that.

Nikki took the next flight of steps two at a time and arrived huffing and puffing at the Hubbs's front door. She took a deep breath, then rang the bell.

"Nikki!" Tyler's mother exclaimed, surprised to see her. "Happy Thanksgiving."

"Good morning, Mrs. Hubbs," Nikki puffed. She could hear the brassy, cheerful sound of the Macy's parade on the television in the front room. "Is Tyler home?"

Mrs. Hubbs frowned and nodded her head sadly.

"He's up in his room, Nikki. Same place he's been for the past four days. Go ahead upstairs, if you want. Maybe you can talk him out of there."

Nikki climbed the short stairway to the second floor. She walked softly down the hall to the door of Tyler's room. Hesitantly, she raised her hand and knocked.

There was no answer.

She knocked again.

"Tyler?"

Nikki turned the knob and pushed the door open. It was dark inside the room, despite the brightness of the day outside. All the shades were down, the lights turned off. Nikki crept into the room and found Tyler slumped in a chair, asleep.

The air smelled odd, somehow. Like the air in a hospital room. Near Tyler's feet lay a cereal bowl, half full of milk. The blankets on his bed were turned down and rumpled and his desktop was littered with cups and saucers. For a moment, she looked at Tyler as he slept, and she felt very glad to see him again. She'd been missing him, just as she'd been missing Hope.

"Tyler," Nikki whispered, touching his arm. "Tyler, wake up."

Tyler woke with a start. He pushed himself forward in the chair, blinking his eyes.

"Nikki?" he said.

"In person," Nikki answered.

"Where's Hope?" Tyler asked immediately, looking all around the chair, even under himself.

"Hope?" Nikki repeated. Pity for Tyler rushed to her heart. Apparently he'd been dreaming and forgotten what had happened. Nikki did not want to have to remind him of the dreadful truth.

"Yes, Hope," Tyler said, jumping up from the chair and turning in dizzy circles as his eyes scanned the darkened room. "She's got to be here somewhere."

"Tyler, what are you saying?" Nikki stood back and watched him. He was certainly not dreaming any longer. "Are you saying that Hope is . . . is alive?"

"Of course she's alive," Tyler returned testily. "I wouldn't be looking for her if she weren't alive, would I?"

"But I thought Dr. Williams said she would have to be put to sleep. I thought—"

"He did," Tyler answered from under his desk. "But he also said there was a small chance of recovery, if someone really wanted to try for it. That was after you left. I tried to call and tell you about it but . . . well, you know . . ."

Nikki nodded, feeling both stupid and guilty. She could hardly believe what she was hearing. She had already faced and accepted the worst, and now Tyler had uttered the sweetest news imaginable. "What am I standing here for?" she suddenly exclaimed, and at that she threw herself on the floor and began crawling about with Tyler, searching for the puppy. Her heart was beating a mile a minute, and she worried that at any moment she herself might wake up from a wonderful dream.

"Ah ha!" Tyler shouted as he peeped into the closet. "There you are, you little rascal."

Nikki opened the door wider so that she too could see inside.

Hope looked up happily and yipped once through a mouthful of canvas tennis shoe.

"Look at that!" Tyler said. "She's up. She's eating! She's getting better! Why, just last night she seemed all but a goner. She wouldn't even take any warm milk. Now look at her!"

Nikki suddenly realized that the bowl of milk by the chair had not been for Tyler's cereal after all. It had been for Hope!

Bright-eyed and mischievous, Hope dropped the tennis shoe and dashed out of the closet toward her bowl of milk.

"It's a miracle!" Nikki said.

"Oh, not really," Tyler answered somewhat pompously. "The doctor told me that if a puppy does get better from distemper it will often happen just as quickly as when it got sick." He snapped his fingers. "Just like that. I've been feeding her mashed dog food from this squeeze tube." Tyler picked up a big plastic syringe from the top of his desk and showed it to Nikki. It was the sort of tube used for basting a turkey.

"She's been eating that?" Nikki said, wrinkling her nose at the smell of the gummy brown stuff inside the tube.

"Better she than me," Tyler answered.

Nikki laughed. Impulsively, she reached forward and squeezed Tyler's arm.

"So you're telling me that you knew all along Hope would get well?" she challenged.

Tyler smiled, reddening a bit. "Actually, I didn't," he admitted. "To tell you the truth, I thought last night that I'd failed for sure."

"But you didn't fail," Nikki said, raising her hand to Tyler's cheek.

"I did mess things up pretty badly, though," Tyler said. "I really am sorry, Nikki."

"Don't try to take all the credit, Tyler. You couldn't have done it without me, you know."

Tyler considered Nikki's point. He smiled, unsurely at first, then with ease as Nikki smiled with him.

Nikki shook her head, amazed at all Tyler had done, and sorry that she hadn't been there to help him. "All this time you've been taking care of Hope," she said, "and I didn't even think you cared. I thought you were only interested in the money."

"Money," Tyler said, and chuckled. "What money? The last of it went toward getting Hope well."

Nikki waved the subject aside. As far as she was concerned, the money could not have been better spent.

"Listen, Nikki," Tyler began uncertainly. "I've had something on my mind these last few days. Aside from Hope, I mean." He walked to his desk, opened a drawer, and withdrew a long sheet of paper. Hesitantly, he held it up for Nikki to see. "How does this sound to you?" he asked, almost in a whisper.

The paper read:

FREE PUPPIES

six in all
males, females
your choice

HAVE you longed for a true friend?
A companion for LIFE?

TAKE OUR PUPPIES, PLEASE!

shots, worming, complimentary bag of Puppy Chow

FREE   **FREE**   **FREE**

Contact Tyler G. Hubbs and/or Nicole S. Savier
south end of playground, after school

SATISFACTION   GUARANTEED

Nikki kept a straight face as she met Tyler's eyes.

"Well?" Tyler said nervously. "Tell me the truth now, Nikki. What do you think? If it's not what you want, I'll think of something else."

"I think it's *wonderful!*" Nikki cried.

And for the first time since she had known him, Nikki threw her arms about Tyler and hugged him tight, squeezing until he groaned and gasped and had to fight to free himself!

26
Hope

By five o'clock on the first Monday after Thanksgiving
vacation five of the puppies had gone to new owners.
Three of the kids Nikki had spoken to at school convinced
their parents to let them have a puppy for keeps. And
the news of the free puppies had spread around school,
so that two more kids showed up unexpectedly to claim
puppies of their own.

Free, as Tyler commented, was a very good price.

One by one, he and Nikki said their good-byes, to
Bluto and Cubby, to Sugar Baby and Caddie, and last,
but not least, to Albert Einstein.

Finally, only Hope remained.

Nikki held the little dog in her arms as she stood by
the window in the front room, gazing out on a clouded
sky which promised rain before nightfall. Hope
squirmed, licked her hands, tried to scale the front of her
sweater.

"We're going to have to get your nails clipped," Nikki
said, unhooking Hope's little claws from the wool. She
heard her own words and frowned. "Someone will have
to, I mean," she added quietly.

Roxanne wandered in from the kitchen, having finished her Gravy Train dinner, and sat down beside Nikki. She panted as she looked up at the last of her puppies. Nikki knelt and let Rox nuzzle and sniff the pup. Hope blinked her eyes and waggled her head as Rox gave her a slobbery kiss on the ear. Nikki giggled softly and petted Roxie's head.

There was a knock on the door and Nikki's heart jumped to her throat. Instinctively, she held Hope more tightly.

"I'll get it," her father called from the hallway.

This is it, Nikki said to herself. This must be it. I've got to be brave.

The front door opened and closed. For perhaps three minutes, the visitor stayed in the hallway. Nikki could just barely hear a whispering of voices.

At last, footsteps approached the front room. Reluctantly, Nikki turned from the window, cradling Hope closely like a precious jewel.

As her eyes fell upon Tyler, Nikki breathed with relief.

"Oh, it's only you," she said.

"Thanks a lot," Tyler answered, though in a jovial tone of voice. "You really know how to make a guy feel important."

"I'm sorry," Nikki said, smiling warmly. "I just thought . . . it might be someone else."

Tyler and Mr. Savier moved to Nikki's side. Both reached between her arms to pet Hope's head.

"So she's still here," Tyler observed. "I was afraid she'd be gone before I got back from my dinner."

"Why doesn't anyone want her?" Nikki wondered aloud. "Hope is such a pretty dog. Such a nice, silvery-gray puppy. I don't understand it."

"I think I do," Mr. Savier said, winking at Tyler. "It seems to me that people might suspect Hope is your favorite when they come to look at the pups."

"Oh?" Nikki said, pretending not to understand.

"You're always holding her," Tyler explained. "Kissing her head, petting her ears. A person would probably feel like a criminal if he tried to take that puppy away from you."

Nikki's cheeks burned. What Tyler was saying was absolutely true. Hope was her favorite, and had been from the start. Nikki just couldn't help loving her. The poor puppy had been through so much.

"I'll try not to be so obvious about it after this," she yielded, setting the puppy on the floor. "You should have said something earlier."

Tyler crouched and scooped up Hope. He touched his nose to hers and laughed when she sneezed and shook her head.

Mr. Savier smiled at Tyler, then put an arm around Nikki's shoulders. He slipped his free hand into the front of his shirt.

"I think you can stop worrying about Hope," he told Nikki. "A very satisfactory parent has already come forth."

"Really?" Nikki said. "Who is it? Do I know the person?"

"I should say so," her father answered. "It seems

that a young man by the name of Tyler Hubbs has expressed a keen interest in adopting this particular dog."

"You?" Nikki exclaimed, turning to Tyler. "But you told me that puppies aren't allowed in your apartment."

"They're not," Tyler admitted. "That's my only problem, Nikki. You see, what I really need, to finalize the deal, is for someone to sort of keep Hope for me."

Nikki stared, openmouthed, at Tyler. He was grinning from ear to ear. She turned her wide eyes to her father. He nodded, smiling just as widely as Tyler.

"If this is truly what you want," he said, "well . . . I guess we can manage one more dog around here."

Tears of joy popped from Nikki's eyes as she stood on her toes and kissed her father's cheek, then turned and accepted Hope from Tyler's outstretched arms. She hugged the dog close, snuggled its soft snout beneath her chin, and giggled as her sandpapery tongue lashed her neck and cheeks.

"Welcome home, Hope," Nikki said, raising the wiggly puppy between herself and Tyler. "Welcome home to your permanent family."